WOULD YOU SETTLE FOR IMPROBABLE?

P. J. Petersen

LAUREL-LEAF BOOKS bring together under a single imprint outstanding works of fiction and nonfiction particularly suitable for young adult readers, both in and out of the classroom. Charles F. Reasoner, Professor Emeritus of Children's Literature and Reading, New York University, is consultant to this series.

Published by
Dell Publishing Co., Inc.
1 Dag Hammarskjold Plaza
New York, New York 10017

Laurel-Leaf Library ® TM 766734,
Dell Publishing Co., Inc.

ISBN: 0-440-99733-X

RL: 5.6

Printed in the United States of America

February 1983

10 9 8 7 6

WFH

FOR KAREN

ONE

FROM THE NOTEBOOKS
Assignment: Describe this school in a paragraph.

ELVIRA PORTALUPE: MARSHALL MARTIN JUNIOR High School, a three-year intermediate school, has a student body of approximately 550. The building originally housed Hendley High School, but it was converted into a junior high school when the senior high was built in 1973. Although the building itself has seen better days, there is much here of which we can be proud. . . .

Jeff Garrison: Marshall Martin is like a jail. You can't go off the schoolgrounds at lunch, even if you have a note from your mother. Which is not fair. If your mother says it's OK for you to go downtown, why doesn't Mr. Bellows let you go?

Dottie Williams: I don't need a paragraph. One sentence is enough—Marshall Martin is BORING!!!

Harry Beech: This is the most run-down school I have ever seen. I don't mind the old beat-up desks or the leaky roof, but I hate it when it gets hot and the cooler doesn't work. That's when I want to

sneak home and watch TV under the air conditioner. To tell you the truth, even on cool days I
would rather stay home and watch the *Dialing
for Dollars* movie. Who wouldn't?

Jennifer Kirkpatrick: Marshall Martin JHS is a
gyp. If we lived in any other town around here,
we would be in high school now. In Hendley, however, they were too chintzy to build a four-year
high school, so we are ninth graders instead of
freshmen. The difference between ninth graders
and freshmen is that freshmen go to games and
rallies and parties while ninth graders stay home
and think about next year.

Michael Parker: Marshall Martin is your average
run-of-the-mill junior high. What can you expect
when you live in an average run-of-the-mill town?
Except for one teacher, I like it here, but that is
probably because I am an average run-of-the-mill
student.

TWO

MONDAY, APRIL 10

THE CLOCK ABOVE THE GYM DOOR READS 2:01, which means that I have three minutes left of pass period. At Marshall Martin we don't have recesses —we have pass periods. The two aren't the same. At recess you're supposed to play. During pass period you're supposed to gather your books, walk quietly to your next classroom, settle yourself at your desk, and sit silently until class begins. That isn't what happens, of course, but that's what is supposed to happen.

Two years ago, when I was a seventh grader, pass period was five minutes long. But our new principal, Mr. Bellows, cut it to four minutes after he discovered that he could walk from metal shop to the science wing (the longest walk in the school) in less than three minutes. He did it when everybody else was in class, though. If he had tried it during a real pass period, he might have let us keep the extra minute.

Still, a lot can happen in four minutes. Barry Barton claims that he left his art class, ran a block and a half down the street to the Circle K store, bought a Freezie, drank it on the way back, and got into his shop class before the bell rang. Barry bragged about it so long that some guys finally called him on it—and they were dumb enough to put up the money for the Freezie. Barry took off after art class, just the way he was supposed to, but he didn't come back until the next day. He claimed that Mr. Bellows saw him leave and chased him down an alley, where he hid in a garbage can. Mr. Bellows supposedly walked right by him but never thought to look inside the can. Barry said he'd try it again if somebody would give him the money for another Freezie, but nobody would.

And there was a story going around that Link Kauffman, the only guy in the ninth grade with a moustache, beat up two different guys during one pass period. He may have taken more than four minutes to do it—the last thing in the world Link would brag about would be getting to class on time.

As I walk past the gym door and head down the corridor past the ninth-grade lockers, Harold Riscotti pushes by me and dashes into the boys' room. "Sorry, Ace," he says. "Nicotine fit." Every pass period he goes into the lavatory for a smoke. Actually, he runs into a stall, locks the door, lights up, takes one puff, and blows smoke all over himself. Then he throws the thing into the toilet. The whole routine takes less than thirty seconds. For some reason, he thinks it's really exciting to walk into class with his clothes stinking of smoke.

I make my way through the traffic jam in front

of the girls' lavatory—a hundred girls with brushes in their hands. The ones who can't get inside the door stand in the hallway working their brushes anyway. Brush, brush, brush, flip. Brush, brush, brush, flip.

Salvador Sanchez dives between two flying hairbrushes and grabs my arm. "Hey, Mike," he says, "what's Old MacDonald's first name?" It's an old joke, but I shake my head. "Old!" he shouts. "Gotcha again." He runs off down the hall.

Ahead of me some seventh-grade boys are playing keep away with somebody's math book. Seventh graders are always playing keep away. They toss the book back and forth until everybody gets tired of that, and then one of them dumps the book into a trash can. When the owner of the book starts digging in the can, the others yell for a teacher. Lots of things change around school, but keep away isn't one of them.

By the drinking fountain there are two guys with their cheeks full of water. They are giggling and threatening to spit it on each other. And they keep trying to slap each other's cheeks. Meanwhile, most of the water dribbles down their chins. Mr. Kelley, in the hallway by his door, is ignoring them.

We used to have hall monitors at Marshall Martin. When I was in the seventh grade, they were called the Hall Safety Patrol. Last year they were the Block M Club. Both years the same thing happened. Most people quit the first week, and the rest only reported little kids.

This year we don't have monitors. The teachers

are supposed to come out of their classrooms and stand there and supervise. Most of them take their time about getting out to the hall, and once they are there, they look up at the ceiling or talk to each other. If you think about it, you can see why. What teacher wants to bother about a couple of morons spitting water on each other?

As I turn the corner by the band room, I can see Ms. Karnisian's head towering above everything else in the crowded hall. Ms. Karnisian is only in her second week of student teaching, so she always comes out of the room right at the beginning of pass period.

The students give her plenty of leeway as they pass her. I've gotten used to her, but she's a little frightening at first. She's the biggest woman I ever saw—both tall and wide through the shoulders, like a football player—and her jaw sticks out like a boxer's. When she first started visiting our English class, Harry Beech said she looked like King Kong. People have been calling her King Kong Karnisian ever since—not to her face, of course.

I didn't know what to think about Ms. Karnisian at first. We had had old Miss Kellaher for the first two thirds of the year, and we hadn't done much except take easy grammar and spelling tests and watch movies. Miss Kellaher used to teach in the high school, but when they built the new high school and made this building into a junior high, they left her behind. She's about ready to retire, and she acts exhausted all the time.

When Ms. Karnisian took over the class, she

started right in making us write and read and even do homework. When some of the kids complained that it wasn't fair, Ms. Karnisian just laughed and said, "Nobody ever said the world was fair. If it was, would I have this face and this body?"

A few of the students refused to do the assignments for a day or two, and Ms. Karnisian just laughed and said that they had a choice, but since they were minors, she wanted to be sure that their parents agreed with their choice. So she put together a little note that said, "I prefer not to learn anything. Therefore I will not do any of the assignments and will sit in my class and stare at my desk each day." She even left a place for the signature of the student. Then, below that, there was another line—"I accept my child's decision" —and a place for the parent to sign. Whenever anybody started to complain about the work, she would hand them a copy of the note. Nobody ever filled one out, of course, except as a joke.

There were other things too. Ms. Karnisian was different from any teacher I ever had. She'd listen to somebody whine about how hard they were trying, and she'd laugh and say, "I don't want you to try. I want you to write. If you do write and some of it's garbage, that's all right. Everybody writes garbage sometimes. But writing garbage is ten times better than trying and not writing anything." And on the first paper I wrote for her, she said that she liked some parts but thought that in one section all I was doing was dirtying paper. I didn't know what to think. Even after I went through and figured out what she meant, I wasn't sure I liked my work being called dirtying paper—even if that's what it was.

Being a student teacher, Ms. Karnisian doesn't get paid. She says she doesn't mind working for free, but she wishes they'd give her gas money. Every day she has to drive to Hendley from San Martin (about fifty miles each way) in her rattle-trap VW. She doesn't let us forget it either. "All right," she'll say, "somebody write something that will make it worth the hundred-mile trip." Or "I just had a flat tire outside of Warner and had to try to change it without getting my clothes dirty. I want you to write something good enough to make me glad I made the trip anyway." And she'll write things on our papers like "A five-mile phrase" or "A twenty-mile sentence," by which she means that the writing is worth driving that far.

Ms. Karnisian is leaning against the wall, reading a book. Just as I go by, she reaches out her foot and pretends she's trying to trip me. I laugh, but it still surprises me. Somehow I don't expect a teacher to do that. "Don't horse around in the hall, Michael," she says, trying to keep a straight face.

I get to class with over a minute to spare. As usual, Warren Cavendish is already there, sitting in the middle seat of the back row, which is where he sits in every class. Warren is almost always the first one to English because he has fifth-period social studies in the room next door. (This piece of scheduling is due to a computer error, according to Warren. He says that each student's schedule is designed so that every class is in a different wing of the building—part of a plot to control the students by tiring them out.)

Warren is the smartest student in the ninth grade, also one of the fattest. He seems older than the rest of us ninth graders, even though he's actually four days younger than I am. He's the kind of person who was born old, if you know what I mean. He moved to Hendley when we were in the fourth grade, and he was already putting together electric motors and solving chess problems.

Warren is talking to Jennifer Kirkpatrick as I come down the aisle. He turns around as I reach my desk. "Michael," he says, "would you care to make a small wager?"

"Probably not."

"I don't know how you find these things out," Jennifer says to Warren. As usual, she plays with her hair while she talks. She has long blond hair that she's always patting and smoothing, like somebody petting a dog.

"You just have to know what to look for," Warren says. "Michael, I'll give you odds of five to one that we have a fire drill this hour."

With all the years I've spent around Warren, I don't even have to wonder. I know he's figured out some way to tell when the drills are coming. He sits there with his superior smile, and I decide not to give him what he wants.

"Why would I want to bet on that?" I ask. "It's obvious we're going to have one."

Warren straightens up in his chair. "What do you mean?"

"Well, everybody knows we're going to have a fire drill, right? Jennifer, you knew we were going to have a fire drill, didn't you?"

"Are you kidding?" Jennifer says.

"You're bluffing," Warren says. "You didn't have any idea we were going to have one until I said so."

"If you want to believe that," I say, "I don't mind."

"Come on, then," says Warren. "How could you tell?"

"It's obvious, isn't it?"

Warren takes out his book as he says, "You are singularly unamusing." He ignores me, but when Margaret Olson comes in, he offers her a twenty-to-one bet.

Margaret groans. "Where were they when I needed them? Why couldn't we have had a drill last period so that I could have missed my gymnastics test?" She turns to me. "I got a D+ on my somersault. A D+! What's a D+ somersault anyway? If you make it all the way over, that ought to count for something. Here's old Margaret Olson —failure—deficient in somersaulting."

"They'll probably let you graduate anyway," I say.

"Not this outfit. I'll probably have to go to summer school and take Remedial Somersaulting."

"Okay, Warren," Jennifer says, "how can you tell? Tell us how you know." Warren just grins.

"It's obvious," I tell her.

The red second hand on the clock is moving

past the ten, and people begin to rush through the door. The bell starts to ring just before the second hand touches the twelve. Harry Beech dives into the room, dropping his books on the floor. Somebody yells, "Nice going, butterfingers." Somebody else says, "When'd you graduate from charm school, Grace?" As Harry scoops up his books, Ms. Karnisian closes the door.

Warren has his hand up immediately. "Ms. Karnisian, were you ever here at Marshall Martin when we had a fire drill?"

"No," she says. "Have I missed something?"

"You can judge for yourself."

Ms. Karnisian looks at him for a second and then starts passing out our notebooks. "Your work is getting better and better. Less flab and more meat. More concrete—" And then the oogah-oogah horns begin blaring. She looks at us, obviously confused. I can't blame her. No place else in the world has horns that sound like those. My house is over a mile from school, and my mother usually knows when we have a fire drill.

"Fire drill!" everybody yells.

We wander out of the classroom and down the corridor to the exit. There's the same kind of traffic jam that we have during pass period, except that nobody is crowded around the lavatories. In fact, the whole thing looks like a pass period in slow motion.

We stand outside the building for five minutes or more. Some of the girls start brushing their hair. While Harry Beech is telling me about a rerun of

Twilight Zone that he saw on TV last night, Warren comes by and says, "Did I tell you, or did I tell you?"

"It was obvious, wasn't it?" I say. He glares at me and wanders off. I enjoy getting to him, but I still can't help wondering how he could tell we were going to have a fire drill. Maybe the janitor does something different.

Finally the bell rings, and we go back inside. As soon as everyone is settled, Ms. Karnisian starts to talk about today's assignment. We know better, but this is her first fire drill. She has just started to read a poem when the chimes sound over the loudspeaker system. Our principal, Mr. Bellows, uses these chimes to announce that he's ready to talk. Because of the chimes, the students call him Ding Dong Bellows.

After a second series of chimes, Mr. Bellows begins: "Students, that wasn't a bad drill. Not a bad drill at all. That was a horrible drill. That was a disgrace. If there had been a real fire, we would have had barbecued mustangs all over this school." (In case you can't tell, the Marshall Martin mascot is the mustang.)

Things follow the usual line after this. There's a second fire drill that doesn't seem to go any better than the first. We have another evaluation, and for a minute I think we're going to have a third drill. So does Ms. Karnisian. "Enough's enough," she says to nobody in particular. "My ears can't take another round of those horns."

By the time things settle down, we only have time to go over our homework and to write in our notebooks. The topic for the day is "How I Differ from Other People My Age." It's a tough topic for me because I don't differ from other people my age. I'm so ordinary I make myself sick.

"The way I differ," Margaret Olson whispers, "is that I do D+ somersaults."

When the bell rings, Ms. Karnisian collects the notebooks and says that she wants to see Warren and Harry and me. Jeff Garrison gives me the old now-you're-in-for-it look, but I'm not worried. Ms. Karnisian isn't the kind to let something go by and then catch up with it later. Harry looks over at Warren and me. "We're not in trouble," he says, but he sounds less sure than he should.

Jennifer and Margaret hang around the front of the room, hoping to find out what's going on, but Ms. Karnisian just smiles and waits for them to leave. Then she comes to the back of the room and sits on a desk. We are standing by this time, leaning against the back wall. With her sitting and us standing, our eyes are almost level.

"I have a favor to ask the three of you," she says. "But I want you to understand that it's strictly a favor. It has nothing to do with class, and you don't have to do it. Just say you'd rather not, and that'll be the end of it."

"I'll do it," Harry says.

Ms. Karnisian smiles. "I like your style, but you'd better wait and see what it is first."

"Okay," Harry says, "but I'll do it."

"Here it is," she says. "I work nights at the county juvenile hall. I don't know if you knew that." We didn't. "I have a title, but my job is to be

a kind of baby-sitter. They need one woman on the
staff in case they have a girl brought in who has
to be searched. We only keep girls there overnight,
though. They also think that a woman can handle
the boys more easily because there isn't the same
challenge that there would be with a male attend-
ant. They wanted a big strong-looking woman
who wasn't too attractive, and for some reason
they hired me instead." I sort of smile at that, but I
don't really think it's funny. It always makes me
uncomfortable when people put themselves down.
"It's a lousy job in some ways, and I don't always
get enough sleep, but I couldn't afford to be a student teacher without it."

I've never seen the juvenile hall, and I can't
picture it. All I can think of is something out of
an old prison movie called *Riot in Cell Block
Eleven*.

"One of my duties," she goes on, "is to supervise the evening study hall. I get to know the boys
pretty well during that time. There's one that I've
spent quite a bit of time with, a boy named Arnold.
When I first started to work there, I got after him
because he just sat night after night and flipped
pages. He showed me what he was supposed to
be doing—a programed course in social studies.
He said the work was too boring and too easy. I
didn't know what else to do, so I gave him one of
my psychology textbooks. He read it all the way
through and then asked me for more. I don't think
he understands everything, but he wants something that challenges him, something that doesn't
boil down to marking the correct box."

I keep listening and watching Ms. Karnisian's face as she talks. Her eyes are different from other people's—livelier, full of fire. When you watch those eyes, you forget about the rest of her face. I keep wondering what the favor is going to be.

"This isn't something I would spread around, but I think it's important for you to understand the situation. Arnold just turned fifteen, and he has been in and out of the county juvenile hall since he was eight. He lives with his mother, and she doesn't have much to offer. When he was little, he was put in the hall whenever she was put in jail. They don't do that anymore, but he's still a regular. He always seems to get into something. He steals, he lies, he cons everybody around him. And nobody knows quite what to do with him."

"Maybe they better keep him locked up," Warren says. "He sounds dangerous." Warren is joking, but Ms. Karnisian nods seriously.

"Actually, you're right. He *is* dangerous, although he's not vicious at all. He's intelligent and totally without direction."

"So what does he have to do with us?" asks Warren.

"Here's the situation. He's going to be released from the hall this weekend. His mother has moved, and she has convinced the powers that be that she's ready to take care of him. Truthfully, I'm not sure that they're convinced of anything. But they don't like to keep him in the hall if they can help it. So he's coming out of the hall and moving to a new town. And, if you try really hard, you can probably guess which one. On Monday morning he'll be here at Marshall Martin."

"Wow," Harry says. "Oh, wow."

"He'll fit right in," Warren says. "What's another hood when you already have fifty?"

"But it doesn't have to work that way, Warren," she says. "If Arnold is ever going to have a chance, this is it. He's in a new town, he's starting fresh, and he's had his fill of juvenile hall. He just might be able to turn things around. He might not, too. But there's a chance anyway. And if it doesn't work, what have we lost?"

"What do you want us to do?" I ask.

"I thought maybe we could all go do something this Saturday. That way Arnold could meet you boys. Nothing big and fancy. It just might help him to start school knowing a few people. It just might make a difference. How does it sound?"

"It sounds impossible," Warren says.

"All right," Ms. Karnisian says, smiling at him. "Thanks for staying after class."

"I didn't say I wouldn't do it," Warren says. "I just said it sounded impossible. I don't mean meeting him—I mean helping him. That's what sounds impossible."

"Would you settle for improbable?" Ms. Karnisian says and then laughs.

Harry and I both say we'll do whatever we can.

"What about the bowling alley?" she asks. "That would give you something to do, but still give you a chance to talk."

"Bowling?" says Warren, as if she has suggested Russian roulette.

"Why not? I'll even pay for it."

"I've never bowled in my life. I don't even know how."

"Then it'll be a new experience for you. Shall we meet at the alley around two? Can you all make it then?"

"I'll show up," Warren says, "but that's all I'm promising."

As the three of us walk out of the room, Harry still wants to talk. "This is kind of neat, you know? This Arnold, he sounds all right."

"Yeah," I say. For some reason, though, I keep thinking about a kid named Jesse Bailey, who was in my third-grade class. I used to feel sorry for him because he never had a lunch. I used to share my sandwich with him, but he'd still get mad at me and beat me up about once a week. I still felt sorry for him, but I was glad when he moved away.

"Bowling," Warren mutters. "Why does it have to be bowling? I'm not going to bowl. I'll go down there, but I'm not going to bowl."

"Who knows?" I say. "Maybe you're a natural. Bowling just might be your sport."

"You are singularly unamusing," Warren says.

THREE

Assignment: How I differ from other people my age

ELVIRA PORTALUPE: IN MOST WAYS I SUPPOSE that I am like others in my age group, but I differ in my general interests. I am much more serious than most people my age. I am more concerned about the future, both my own and that of the world. Therefore I believe that education should be taken seriously. . . .

Jeff Garrison: I can play pinball better, shoot pool better, and play Ping-Pong better than other people my age. If I wasn't such an honest guy, I could be a hustler. (Some people would say that I'm better looking than other guys my age, but I wouldn't want to sound conceited.)

Dottie Williams: I am more mature than most girls my age. The things that interest junior high girls are boring to me. All of the people here at Marshall Martin, especially the boys, seem like children. . . .

Margaret Olson: Although I may look like other ninth graders, don't be fooled. I am really a vampire. At night I rise from my coffin and go out searching for blood. It is hard to get your homework done when you are a vampire, as you are very busy after dark. And then with school every day, you get very little sleep. However, every job has its drawbacks.

Harry Beech: I get to stay up as late as I want to. So I can watch all the horror movies that come on TV, even the ones that start at eleven o'clock. I have to get up and go to school, though, no matter how late I stay up.

I can have anything to eat that I want because I do most of the shopping and cooking. I can go anywhere I want, as long as I tell my dad first. My dad doesn't watch TV, so I can watch anything I want. I guess I'm luckier than other people my age.

Jennifer Kirkpatrick: One way I'm different is that my parents think I'm still five years old. They are very, very strict about where I go and what I do. Whenever I begin to ask about dating, it ends up with my father shouting, "We will do what we think is best for you, and I don't want to hear any more about it."

Another way that I'm different is that I have to be on a diet all the time. All I have to do is look at a candy bar and I put on three pounds. While other people are stoking up on junk food, I am slowly starving. And I am the one with the big waistline.

*   *   *

Michael Parker: I don't really differ from other people my age. I am so average that it's sickening. Everything about me is right down the middle. Just to give you an idea, there are fifteen boys in my home room that are taller than I am and fifteen that are shorter. I know because we had to line up by height for yearbook pictures. I live in an average house in an average part of town with my average family—one sister and a dog. My dog is much easier to get along with than my sister, but that's normal too.

My friends are the only thing about me that can't be called average, but that doesn't really count. Part of the reason I like them is that they're different. Take Warren Cavendish. He's the smartest kid in school. He's an only child, and he's never had a pet. (Allergies.) So he's anything but average. Or look at Harry Beech. He lives with his father in a trailer and watches monster movies all the time. Or Salvador Sanchez. He's the oldest of eight children, and he can speak both Spanish and English.

But me? I am typical, average, normal, and blah.

Warren Cavendish: This is too easy. I am smarter, fatter, and more obnoxious. I am the oddball kid of oddball parents. My father has the longest beard in Hendley, and my mother is a dentist. A foot-long beard is strange enough in a town like this, but nobody's mother is supposed to be a dentist. She likes her work, though, and people say she is very good.

Even though my parents don't fit in with most people in Hendley and don't really want to, they hope that I can fit in. When the counselors tried to move me into high school last year, my parents refused. They say that I can study whatever I like outside of school but that they want me to go through a normal school situation. They were afraid I would be a freak at the high school. What they don't realize is that I'm a freak here anyway.

The stupid thing is that I end up making myself more of a freak than I have to. I brag too much and try to sound really smart at the times when I am feeling the dumbest. (That is called "over-compensation," but what good does it do to know what to call it if you keep on doing it?)

FOUR

SATURDAY, APRIL 22

AT TWO O'CLOCK WARREN, HARRY, AND I ARE LEAN-
ing against the ball racks at the bowling alley,
waiting for Ms. Karnisian. The whole building
seems to be vibrating with noise. Usually Saturday
afternoon would be a quiet time, but we've picked
the day when a group called Parents Without
Partners is having a bowling party. It's amazing
how many parents in our town don't have partners. There are four or five people on each alley,
and swarms of little kids are running back and
forth between the scoring tables and the snack
bar.

"She'd better hurry," Harry says. "There's only
one lane left."

"Maybe we ought to get it," I say. "We could get
it and then not bowl until she gets here."

"Don't bother," Warren tells us. "I don't want to
bowl anyway."

"You might like it," I say. "You never tried it."

"I've never been run over by a steamroller
either, but I don't have to try it to know how I
feel about it."

We talk about playing the pinball machines,

but the PWPs have all of the machines going, even the Mississippi River machine that nobody ever plays because it always tilts on the fourth ball. Harry wanders off, saying that he'll get us each a Coke.

Warren and I find an empty bench and sit down. Two little girls run around the bench, hiding behind us and playing some kind of peekaboo game. "The whole thing is ridiculous," Warren moans. "The more I think about it, the more ridiculous it gets. What are we doing here anyway?"

"We're going bowling. It's no big deal."

"Yeah, but why are we going bowling? So that we can meet this jailbird and make friends with him."

"You didn't have to come."

Warren leans back on the bench and looks at the ceiling. "I have two questions for you, Michael. Take them in the order you like. First, do you really want some kid who has spent half his life in juvenile hall for your friend? Especially when you know that he's a cheat and a thief and a liar? Are you going to be able to keep from checking your wallet every time he goes by? Question two: Do you really think he'd want you as his friend? Or me? Or Harry? Go ahead. Answer either of those."

"Come on," I say. "He's just a guy our age. He's not Jesse James."

The little girls who have been running around the bench now start to crawl under it. They climb over our feet and through our legs until we finally

get up and move, which is probably what they
wanted all along. As soon as we leave, they climb
on the bench and start walking back and forth
as though they're on a tightrope.

Warren leans against the ball rack again.
"What you and I are involved in, Michael, is something called peer influence. Do you know what
that is?"

"No." I have kind of an idea, but it's easier to
play dumb.

"A peer is an equal, but the term is generally
used to mean people of your own age group. We
are to be good influences on the jailbird's char-
acter. Through his acquaintance with us, he will
turn away from his life of crime and live a good
and noble life. Everyone will live happily ever
after."

"Warren, you make me sick."

"Face it, Michael. Isn't that what this is all
about?"

"Why didn't you stay home? Nobody made you
come."

"Why should I? The whole thing may be interesting. I was just pointing out what kind of a
half-baked operation we have going. Ms. Karnisian
is trying to do the impossible. Improbable, she
calls it. But it's King Kong against the world—
just like in the movie. You've seen it. You know
how it goes. That big gorilla keeps fighting and
fighting, but it's hopeless from the start. He can
knock down a plane or two, but there's no way
he can beat the whole world. And that's what he's
up against. You sit and watch, and you keep

hoping that he can make it, but down deep you know it's a lost cause."

"You'll be a lot of help, I can tell."

"Don't worry about me. I'll do what I can. They probably won't show up anyway. The jailbird probably won't want to be seen with Ms. Karnisian."

We stand around for a while and watch people bowl. One little girl carries her ball to the front line, sets it down on the floor, then gives it a push with both hands. The ball looks as if it will stop halfway down the alley, but it wobbles all the way down to the pins. "Keep your eye on her," I tell Warren. "Maybe you'll pick up some pointers."

Harry comes back with three paper cups of Coke. "I can't believe that woman. Twenty people in line, and she doesn't move one bit faster than she does when she's by herself." He hands us each a cup. "Do you think we ought to get a lane?"

"It doesn't matter," I say. "Some of these people seem to be finishing."

"Harry," Warren says, "do you know why we're here?"

"Sure," Harry answers. "Free bowling." He tips up his cup and looks away. Warren lets it go. I stand there and wonder why I can't handle things that easily.

The PWP bowling party is beginning to break up—not soon enough, though. A little boy has his arms wrapped around his mother's leg and is sobbing. Another boy is sitting on the floor crying. A girl who is a seventh grader at Marshall Martin is arguing with her mother and taking off her shoes and saying that she doesn't even want to finish the game. People are heading for the main desk in a hurry.

"This is really exciting," Warren mutters. Harry and I ignore him.

"You know what's on *Creature Features* tonight?" Harry asks. "*House of Wax.*"

"I've seen it," I say.

"Me too," Harry says. "Six times. It's neat."

It's almost three o'clock when Ms. Karnisian comes through the door. She smiles at us, but it's the kind of smile that looks like it takes effort. We look around, but she seems to be alone.

"Sorry, boys," she says. "Sometimes it works, and sometimes it doesn't. Arnold's out in the car, but he's decided he doesn't want to bowl. Don't ask me why, because I don't know. He told me two weeks ago that he loved to bowl. Anyway, I'm sorry we're so late. Do you want to go ahead and bowl, or would you like to get some ice cream at the snack bar?"

I'd like to bowl, but of course I say that ice cream will be great. Ms. Karnisian goes off to see if Arnold will join us, while the three of us head for the snack bar.

There is a line of people at the bowling counter, and the man at the cash register is running through score sheets as fast as he can. One girl is yanking on her mother's hand and saying, "But I want to go to pizza. Please. Please, please. Please, please, please." Her mother shakes her hand loose without looking down.

We get one of the two tables at the snack bar

and move a fifth chair over. Before anyone takes our order, Ms. Karnisian comes in, with a dark-haired guy walking about three steps behind her. "There's our man," Warren says.

Arnold has his thumbs hooked in his pockets, and he walks along as if he is expecting somebody to jump on his back any second. His hair is long and a little curly, and it covers up part of his face. His shirt is unbuttoned down to his stomach, and his pants are hanging in the danger zone—one bad move and they'll be around his ankles. There is something about his eyes that makes me uncomfortable, but I can't figure what it is—something cold and far away. Even when he looks at you, he doesn't seem to see you. It's as if he's looking at something three feet behind you.

Ms. Karnisian gives me another tired smile and hands me a ten-dollar bill. "Michael, you be treasurer, all right? I have to do a couple of things downtown. I'll be back in an hour or so." She turns and walks away, leaving the three of us sitting there looking at Arnold.

"Sit down," I say, trying to be as friendly as I can.

He shrugs and says, "Why not? It's too wet to plow." He slides down into a chair.

We sit and look at each other for a minute until Harry says, "I'm Harry. This is Warren and Mike."

"Yeah," Arnold says. "One of you guys got a smoke?" We all shake our heads. "I figured as much."

"Is a banana split all right with everybody?" Harry asks. "If we wait for her to come over here, we'll starve to death." Warren and I say all right, and Arnold shrugs. Harry gets up and goes to the counter.

"You guys go to Marshall Martin, huh?" Arnold asks, as though he doesn't care much one way or the other.

"That's right," I say.

"Tell me, man. You got any action at Marshall Martin?"

I look over at Warren to see if he's going to answer. He isn't. He is looking off in another direction. I don't know what to say. I'm not sure what Arnold means by action, but I think that there is probably a shortage of it at Marshall Martin. "Some," I say. "Not too much."

Arnold snorts. "I'll bet. I'll just bet."

We wait. Arnold has nothing more to say. Warren is leaning back in his chair, staring at the ceiling. When I can't stand the silence any longer, I say, "When do you start school?"

Arnold looks at me disgustedly. "Come on, man. You trying to spoil my appetite?"

After that, the silence doesn't seem so bad.

Harry comes back with two banana splits, sets them down, grabs the ten dollars, and goes back for the others. We just sit and look at them. There is probably a banana somewhere, but I can't see it. All I can see is a huge mound of whipped cream with a cherry on top.

"I don't know about you guys," Harry says, setting one of the dishes in front of Arnold, "but I'm hungry." He sits down and attacks his dish. The rest of us do the same. Arnold takes a while to get started, but he polishes his off as quickly as the rest of us. When he is finished, he runs a finger around the dish to get the last of the syrup.

"So this is the big action in Hendley, huh? Banana splits at the bowling alley?"

I look at Harry and Warren as we all shrug. Warren is getting his I-told-you-so look on his face.

After a long minute, Harry asks, "Have you ever seen *House of Wax*?"

"What about it?"

"It's on TV tonight."

"That's it for around here, huh? Bowling alleys and banana splits and TV. That's the big action in this hot town, huh? What do you do for big celebrations—play jump rope?"

Warren stands up and pushes back his chair. "I find you singularly unamusing," he says to Arnold. "Your manners are as slovenly as your conversation is monotonous." With that, he turns and walks away.

Arnold stares after him. "What did that fat turkey say?"

"I couldn't repeat it if you paid me," Harry says.

Arnold comes close to laughing, as close as he has come so far. "I ought to write that down and learn it." He turns around and looks at Warren, who is standing by the pinball machines. "Did he make that up?"

"Sure," Harry says. "He's a genius, kind of. He talks like that any time he feels like it."

"Any time he wants to be a pain," I say, but Arnold doesn't pay any attention. He keeps watching Warren.

"Tell you what, man," Arnold says to Harry. "Old Hatchetface gave us ten bucks, right?" Harry nods. "Well, man, let's take some of that change and get a pack of smokes. If we don't, I'm gonna die right here at this table."

"It's not my money," Harry says. "When Ms. Karnisian comes back, ask her."

Arnold gets up from the table. "Forget it, creep. They might take away your Brownie badge." He pushes his chair aside and walks off.

"Well," Harry says to me, "it was a good banana split anyway."

Harry and I wander over to watch the bowlers again. Arnold stands about twenty feet away and chews on a toothpick that he has found somewhere. I keep an eye on the door, hoping to see Ms. Karnisian come back.

When the door finally swings open, Margaret Olson and Jennifer Kirkpatrick walk in. For a minute I'm surprised, but then I start thinking. "Harry," I ask, "did you say anything about Arnold to Jennifer and Margaret?"

"Not much. Why?"

"Turn around."

Harry turns and says, "Oh, wow, I guess I said more than I should have."

Jennifer and Margaret come right over to us, but they're looking around the whole time. It's obvious they haven't come to the bowling alley on Saturday afternoon to see Harry and me. "How's it going?" Jennifer says. She reaches back and pulls on her hair.

Margaret says, "Hey, hey, hey," doing her Fat Albert imitation.

As soon as Arnold sees the girls, he moves over toward us. "Now this is more like what the doctor ordered," he says. He looks at Jennifer and grins. "You never know who you're going to run into at the bowling alley."

"Arnold," I say, "this is Jennifer and Margaret." The girls smile and say hi.

"So what's happening?" Arnold says to them.

"Same old things," Jennifer says. "Not much and nothing."

Arnold laughs out loud. "Right," he says. "Same old things. You look like somebody I used to know, but I can't think who it is."

"I hate to think," Jennifer says.

Margaret looks at me, and we walk away toward the main desk. "So that's the guy Harry was talking about?"

"That's Arnold," I say. "Were you expecting something different?"

"I don't know. I guess I was. I thought guys only wore their shirts unbuttoned when they had hair on their chests."

"Ouch."

"Don't pay any attention to me. I had to say that. I've been incredibly nice all day, and I've had all this nastiness bottled up. I just had to let it go once. Is he all right? You know what I mean. Is he nice?"

"I don't know yet. If he is, he's hiding it pretty well."

Margaret and I talk for a while, but most of the time we're watching Arnold and Jennifer. Arnold is alive for the first time since I've seen him. He waves his hands, laughs, dances around in a circle. Jennifer stands and smiles and plays with her hair.

"I'd better go rescue her," Margaret says finally.

"She looks like she's enjoying it."

"Oh, she is. That's the trouble. I'd better get her out of here before she asks him to marry her. She was ready to fall in love with him before she ever saw him."

When Margaret and I come back, Jennifer says, "I have to go now. We just stopped by for a second. Maybe I'll see you again." She keeps staring into Arnold's eyes.

Margaret elbows me. "We're just in time."

"Hey," Arnold says, "maybe I'll see you on Monday. If they let me out of jail on time."

"Right," Margaret says. She waves to me as they go out the door.

"Hey, man," Arnold says, "that's better. I'm glad to see you got some women in this town. That little blonde's kind of cute. I mean, man, I've seen better, but I've seen a whole lot worse. Know what I mean?"

"Right," I say.

"Where'd the fat turkey go anyway?"

"Warren? He's still over by the pinball machines."

"Is he mad at me? I mean, what'd I do to him?"

"I don't know," I say. "Go ask him."

Arnold moves casually toward the pinball machines, ending up next to Warren. I follow along because there's nothing else to do. Harry is suddenly beside me. "What's he doing now?"

"He wants to talk to Warren. I think he wants to see if Warren is for real."

"I always wondered about that myself," Harry says.

Arnold tries to get Warren's attention, but Warren keeps watching the machines. Finally Arnold says, "Hey. Hey, Warren."

Warren turns and looks at him. "Are you talking to me?"

Arnold starts to say something but stops. Then he says, "This guy says you're a genius."

"How would he know? He's hardly the one I'd select for a judge of geniuses."

Arnold thinks about this for a minute and then laughs. "If you're a genius, how come you're still in junior high school?"

Warren looks at him for a minute as if he's trying to decide whether such a stupid question deserves an answer. "It has been determined," he says slowly, "that advancing a child beyond his chronological peers is generally detrimental to his social and psychological development." He stops for a minute. "In other words, they think it's better for me to be with people my own age. It's only a theory, though. I turned out weird anyway."

Arnold looks at Warren and shakes his head. "How much do you weigh?"

"You must take gross lessons," Warren says. "Nobody could be that crude without special instruction. You ask a fat guy how much he weighs?

Would you ask somebody in a wheelchair if he would ever walk again? Would you ask a one-armed man how he ties his shoes?"

Arnold shrugs and turns to Harry. "You think Hatchetface could spare us a quarter for pinball?"

"I have a quarter," I say. He takes it as if it belonged to him in the first place.

He puts the quarter in the Aladdin machine and runs his hands up and down the sides. He works the flippers several times and twists his head around—the kind of loosening up that some showboat baseball players go through before going up to the plate. "I don't know," he says. "I'm not sure I can play one of these things without a smoke."

From across the room you'd figure Arnold for a pinball shark. He has all the twists and flips and body English that the really good players have. But somehow he doesn't score any more points than most run-of-the-mill players (like me) do, and the game is over in a hurry. When the last ball slides past the flippers, he punches the button for the second game.

"Hold it," Warren says. "Hold it right there."

Arnold turns around and looks at him. "What's your problem, man?"

"You had your game," Warren says. "Give somebody else a chance."

Arnold leans back against the machine. "Hey, man, what's it to you? Was that your quarter that went into the machine?"

Arnold has his fists clenched, but Warren just

looks bored. "If memory serves me, it wasn't your quarter either."

I've had enough. "Let it go," I say. "It was my quarter, and it's no big deal."

"Who needs it?" says Arnold. He glares at us and walks away from the machine. "This must be the turkey capital of the world."

"Nice going," I say to Warren. "What difference did it make?"

"You wouldn't understand anyway," Warren says and marches off.

"Well," Harry says to me, "somebody has to play this game, and it might as well be us."

Harry and I are still playing pinball when Ms. Karnisian comes in. Harry goes on with the game while I take her change to her. She's still smiling, and it's still an effort.

"Did you get your ice cream?"

"We sure did. I hope you didn't mind buying banana splits. They were very good."

"I'm glad to hear it. I didn't really expect any change. Where's Arnold?"

"Over watching the bowlers, I think. He's a little tired of us, I guess."

"And vice versa, no doubt," she says and smiles. This time her smile doesn't seem to take any effort.

"He's all right."

"He's a pain, Michael. Especially today. But we knew he would be. If he was sweet and cooperative, he wouldn't be in the situation he's in."

I'm sorry that things haven't gone better, and I'm sorry that Ms. Karnisian has wasted her Saturday on an idea that turned out to be a bomb. "It wasn't all as bad as it looks right now," I tell her. "We had a good banana split, and we had a pretty good talk."

"Don't worry, Michael," she says. "I wasn't looking for a miracle. Not a quick one anyway."

FIVE

TUESDAY, APRIL 25

AFTER FINISHING OUR LUNCHES, WARREN, HARRY, and I wander out of the cafeteria. The usual teams of guys are playing basketball on the blacktop courts, and the usual circles of girls are crowded along the edge of the blacktop. Unless a ball bounces into the middle of the girls, the two groups have nothing to do with each other. But the girls sit there and talk about how cute this guy or that guy is, and the basketball players are yelling and taking all these fancy shots to show off.

Except for the basketball players, nobody is moving very fast. The noon sun is warm, and each of the scraggly trees on the playground has a clump of people beneath it.

"There's Arnold," Harry says.

"Where?"

"Over there, holding up the building."

Arnold is leaning against the gym, his feet a good distance from the wall, his shoulders and head against it. He has his thumbs hooked in the pockets of his low-hanging jeans, and he's looking over the grounds without moving anything but his eyes.

"Shall we go over and talk to him?" I ask.

Warren snorts. "Why? Haven't you had your recommended daily allowance of insults?"

"We could just say hello."

"Go right ahead. I have better things to do."

"Come on, Warren," I say. "We'll just say hello."

"Be my guest. I tried to talk to him several times yesterday and twice today. It's a waste of time right now. Give him a few days. He may get tired of being by himself."

"He's in my math class," Harry says, "and he keeps telling everybody he just got out of juvie hall. We're doing some problems this morning, and he yells out, 'We didn't do 'em this way when I was in jail.'"

"Let's go over there anyway," I say. "We can just say hello and go on."

"Be my guest," Warren says. "I'll see you later."

Harry and I walk toward the gym, stopping once to hear a bad joke from Salvador Sanchez. Arnold watches us come, but he doesn't say anything to us.

"Hi, Arnold," I say.

"What do you say, Arnold?" Harry says.

"Yeah," Arnold grunts, looking past us.

I start to move past, but Harry stops. "How are things going?"

"Same old garbage," Arnold says. He keeps looking away, as if something interesting is about to happen across the yard.

"How are your classes?" Harry asks.

"Come on, man. Same old garbage. What do you think?"

"That's what I figured," Harry says. "I just thought I'd ask. I thought if you found a good class, maybe I could transfer into it."

Arnold looks away and doesn't answer. I'm ready to move on, but Harry keeps standing there, kicking gravel with his foot. "Hey, man," Arnold says, "what's the best way to sneak out of here?"

"There isn't any," I say.

"Oh, come on, man. This lousy playpen, there's gotta be a way to go over the fence so you don't get caught."

"Take a look around," Harry says. "If a teacher stands up there by the main building—right where Mr. Fernandez is standing right now—he can see every foot of the fence. It was built that way on purpose."

"This is some hot school. Things weren't half this bad in juvie."

"You want to get out of here at noon," Harry goes on, "your mother or dad has to show up at the attendance office. They won't even let you go with a note."

"This place is a real hole—you know that? I've been to crummy schools, but this is the worst I've seen."

"Don't worry, Arnold," Harry says. "You want to get out of here at noon, I got two foolproof ways."

"Yeah?" Arnold sounds interested, but he still keeps leaning against the wall and staring out at the schoolyard.

"Sure. All you have to do is stand right here and light up a cigarette. Pot's even better, but a plain old cigarette will do. You'll be out of here in five minutes. You want to hear the other way?"

"Forget it, man," Arnold says. For a minute I think he is going to smile.

"The side gates are only closed at noon hour," I tell him. "The rest of the time they're open for delivery trucks. Sometimes nobody's watching them. That's how Barry Barton gets away—or so he claims."

"And I suppose you sneak off all the time?" Arnold says.

"No," I say. "But some guys have done it."

"But you never tried it?"

"No. It's a dumb move. Even if you get through the gate without anybody seeing you, they take roll in every class, and the attendance office will know that you were gone. So you get in trouble all the same."

"Oh, mercy me," Arnold says in this sissy voice, "we wouldn't want to get in trouble, would we?" He comes out with a nasty laugh. "You crack me up. I'll bet you were a Boy Scout. I'll just bet you were."

I turn away. As a matter of fact, I belonged to the Boy Scouts for a year, but the troop leader quit, and we had to disband because nobody else would take the job.

Harry looks at me and starts telling about a program he saw last night on *Night Gallery*. Arnold ignores us.

I interrupt Harry in the middle of the program because Link Kauffman is headed toward us. There are ten or fifteen people following him, and more are trotting across the grounds to join in. Whenever Link decides to have a fight, he always spreads the word first. I guess he likes to work in front of an audience.

"Look out," I tell Arnold. "That guy is Link Kauffman. He's always fighting somebody."

"No sweat, man. He doesn't scare me any."

I look the other way, but I don't see anybody in that direction that Link would be interested in fighting. "I think he's after you."

"You just run and hide, Mickey," Arnold says. "I wouldn't want you to get bad dreams from seeing all the blood."

"Hey," Link yells. "Hey, you. I want to talk to you."

Arnold continues to lean against the building. He yawns and stares up at the sky.

"Hey!" Link marches toward Arnold. "I'm talking to you."

Arnold slowly turns his head toward Link. "So?"

Link stops two steps away from Arnold. "You ain't so tough. Just because you been in juvie, that don't make you tough."

Arnold looks at him and yawns again. "I guess you got it figured out then. Congratulations."

"Listen," Link says, reaching out and pushing Arnold, "I could whip you without even trying." He pushes Arnold's shoulder twice more.

Arnold moves his feet, but he keeps his hands

at his sides. "Hold on now, sport," he says. "Let me figure this thing out. You want to fight me—is that right? Or have I got something mixed up?"

"That's right," Link says, pushing him again. "You're not so tough. I could whip the whole juvie hall if I felt like it."

"Do you mean one at a time or all at once?" Arnold asks, half grinning. "I was just kind of wondering."

Link pushes him harder. "Come on, you chicken. Let's see you swing on me. Come on."

"I'd hate to do that," Arnold says. "This is Be Kind to Animals Week." Some of the people in the crowd start to laugh, and Link whirls around with his fists doubled up. The laughter dies out in a hurry.

Link turns back to Arnold and shoves him against the building. "Come on, you chicken. Let's see how tough you are."

"Is that the best you can do, man?" Arnold says, his hands still at his sides. "Big guy like you—you can't shove any harder than that?"

Link pushes him against the building again. "How 'bout that?"

"That's a little more like it, man," Arnold says, grinning as he straightens up. "It was nothing to brag about, but it wasn't too bad."

By this time half the school is crowded around, and there isn't a teacher in sight. "Come on, you chicken," Link says. "Let's go."

"You feel like fighting, man, go ahead," Arnold says in an easygoing voice. "Nobody's stopping you. You go ahead and hit me for a while, and if you hurt me, then maybe I'll hit you back."

Link looks at Arnold for a minute and then hauls off and punches him alongside the head. Arnold goes crashing back against the building, but he manages to smile as soon as he catches himself. "That's a pretty good one. I mean, man, you're no Muhammad Ali, but you're trying anyway." He keeps his hands at his sides as he steps toward Link. "You better try again."

Link pulls back a fist and glares at Arnold. "Come on," he yells.

Arnold stands in front of him, still smiling. "I can't help it, man. You gotta hit me harder than that before I can get in the mood to fight."

Link lets the fist go, knocking Arnold backward. Arnold's knees buckle, but he doesn't fall. "You're getting there, man."

I look across the yard for a teacher, but nobody's coming. As I turn back, Warren pushes past me and steps between Link and Arnold. Link tries to push Warren aside, but Warren holds onto Link's arms. Link shakes loose and grabs the front of Warren's shirt. "It's all right, Link," Warren says. "He's new here at Marshall Martin. He didn't know you were the toughest guy in school."

Link looks at Warren and lets go of his shirt. "He'd better know it now."

"I think he does," Warren says. "Besides, there's a teacher coming."

"He better wise up," Link says. He turns around and marches away. The crowd moves back and lets him go through. Mr. Fernandez is running toward us, but there's nothing left to see.

"No sweat," Arnold says to Warren. "That big clown didn't scare me any."

"You're welcome," Warren says and walks off.

Arnold stands and watches him go. "You know what?" he says to Harry. "That fat turkey's something else. Did you see him come waddling right into the middle of it?"

SIX

FROM THE NOTEBOOKS
Assignment: What I have been thinking about lately

ELVIRA PORTALUPE: I HAVE BEEN THINKING about the coming summer. I am compiling a list of books to read, and I hope to spend my summer furthering my education. If you have any suggestions, I will be very happy to add them to my list. . . .

Jeff Garrison: I have been thinking about graduating from this school. In just a few more weeks I will be all done with Marshall Martin. At the high school they don't have loudspeakers in the rooms, and the kids can go off the schoolgrounds at noon if they want to. The first noon I'm at the high school, I think I'll walk down here and wave at all the prisoners inside the fence.

Jennifer Kirkpatrick: I have been thinking about the idea that opposites attract. It's funny. Sometimes people who are very different feel something toward each other from the first time they meet. . . .

Michael Parker: (CONFIDENTIAL) I have been thinking about Arnold. They might as well take him back to juvenile hall right now. He's just begging to go. He borrowed my pen yesterday, and when I asked him for it, he said he already gave it back. Now he's over at his desk writing with it. And he's just waiting for me to go over there and say something.

I have tried to get along with him, even though he's been rotten to me from the start. Sometimes he won't be too bad. And then, all of a sudden, he'll go after me. Yesterday he said to me right out of the blue: "I bet you live in a subdivision. I bet you have a dog and a color TV and two cars and a fireplace and a barbecue out in the back." So what was I supposed to say? He was right except for the barbecue (my father thinks that barbecuing is a waste of time and good meat), but why should Arnold get mad at me for those things?

Arnold Norberry: I have been thinking about getting out of this lousy place. What a creepy setup. This little town is nowhere, and this school is about as exciting as Juvie Hall. The only thing I like better here is that I don't have to sit in study hall from seven to nine every night with somebody bugging me all the time. I'm not mentioning any names.

SEVEN

THURSDAY, APRIL 27

"JUST ONE MORE DAY," MARGARET OLSON SAYS as she comes down the aisle. "One more day, and we're through with gymnastics. I don't care what the next unit is. I'll even be glad for field hockey. Just so I'm done with gymnastics."

"That bad, huh?" I say.

"Worse. Today I got a D+ for the vault, and that's my best event. Tomorrow is the balance beam, and I keep falling off. Not when I'm trying to do a trick. I fall off while I'm just standing there. And Mrs. Cousins thinks the reason I do so terrible is that I'm not trying. So I don't even get points for effort, the way the other klutzes do."

"Margaret," Jennifer whispers, motioning her to the back of the room.

"True Confessions time again," Margaret says as she goes.

"Here comes Joe Cool," Warren says. "I wonder if his chest ever gets cold."

I look up as Arnold comes down the aisle. After watching him for a few days, I have figured out that he has two basic walks—the stalk and the glide. When he is acting tough, he uses the stalk.

He looks like a cat after its kill then—every muscle tense, head held straight. At other times he goes into a glide, where all of his joints seem to be ball bearings. It's a kind of dance without music.

Today Arnold is gliding. He stares at Dottie Williams and laughs when she turns away. He tosses his books on the desk and sinks into his seat. "Hey, Mickey," he says, turning sideways so that he can see me, "what's that little redhead's name?"

"Dottie Williams," I say. "And my name is Mike."

"No, it isn't. It's Mickey. Like Mickey Rooney and Mickey Mouse." He leans forward. "Hey, Dottie. Dottie."

Dottie turns around. "Are you speaking to me?"

"How's it going, Dottie?"

Dottie looks at him for a minute, then rolls her eyes toward her forehead and faces the front again. Arnold laughs and turns back to me. "Hey, Mickey, is she always that stuck up?"

"That was friendly," I say. "You ought to see her when she's acting stuck up."

"Who needs it, man? I got no time for slime."

Ms. Karnisian starts passing out the notebooks as the last of the students come through the door. Arnold gets his notebook and opens it, then turns back to me.

"Hey, Mickey, do you guys do this notebook business every day?"

"Just about."

"How come? What good does it do?"

"Ms. Karnisian says it's practice—getting used to putting our ideas on paper."

"How come you write so much? I see you just scribbling away the whole time. What do you get out of it?"

"That's what you're supposed to do. You just write along. You don't try to figure out what to say. You just let it come."

Arnold glares at me and uses this sissy voice to say, "That's what you're supposed to do." Then he laughs. "You're unreal—you know that? Lemme see your book."

"Nothing to look at," I say.

"Come on. Lemme see it."

I stick my notebook under my binder. "It's private."

"Private? Don't hand me that. Old Hatchetface reads it every day. How can it be private?"

"It's just stuff I wrote for myself. I don't want anybody else to read it."

"Forget it, turkey. I was just trying to make you feel good. There's nothing you could write in your little notebook that I want to read."

During the first part of class we are talking about making choices—something Ms. Karnisian calls ethics. We start in by listing the best and worst jobs we ever had. Then we have to decide whether we would rather work at the best job for a dollar an hour or the worst job for four dollars an hour. The best job I ever had was mowing Mr. McDaniel's lawn with his riding mower; the worst was washing windows. It takes me all of three seconds to decide that I'd rather mow the lawn for less money.

All through this I can hear Arnold mumbling and muttering, but I can't tell what he is saying. Once he says, "Man, this is dumb," loud enough for the whole class to hear.

About half the class will do the good job for a dollar an hour. Most of the rest have decided that the money's more important. A few people just won't make up their minds. After Ms. Karnisian talks about the values involved—doing what we like versus making money—all the people who chose money want to explain. "Heck," Jeff Garrison says, "if I work a little while at four bucks an hour, then I can do anything I want, and I'll have the money to do it." The ones who chose money start clapping.

"This is dumb," Arnold says out loud. "Nobody's gonna pay ninth graders four bucks an hour to do anything. You're lucky if you can find a job at all. So this is just a crummy waste of time."

"Could be," Ms. Karnisian says. "But you weren't doing anything else anyway. Maybe you'll like some of the other problems better."

"I doubt it," Arnold says.

Ms. Karnisian just smiles and says, "If you get bored, you can always go pay Mr. Bellows a visit." Then she goes on with the class. "New problem. I want you to think of the possession you have that you like the most. It should be an actual thing that you can see and touch—not something like your life or your faith. And pick out something that isn't alive. A stereo, a bike, a ring—whatever you like."

While I write down "my bike," I look over at Arnold. He is leaning back in his chair and staring at the ceiling.

"All right," Ms. Karnisian says. "Here's the situation. You are in a building which has just caught fire. Down the hall to the right is the room where you have left the possession you wrote down. In the opposite direction, down another hall, you hear a dog barking. Which way do you run? Do you go for your possession, or do you try to help an unknown dog? Which way do you go?"

There are hands in the air all over the room, mostly belonging to dog lovers. After a few people have talked, Arnold yells out, "This is crazy. Think about it. If the place was on fire, I'd run out the door and leave 'em both there. And so would anybody else with good sense." The whole class laughs, including Ms. Karnisian.

We go through some more of these problems— little ones like what you would do if you found a wallet with money in it, and big ones like whether you should try to stop somebody dying of cancer from committing suicide. Arnold doesn't seem to pay much attention. He doesn't write anything down, although he mutters a lot about all of this being phony pretend stuff.

We end up talking about ethical problems that people our age might have to solve: What do you do if you've promised to go somewhere with one

person and then somebody else offers something much more interesting? Do you let somebody copy the homework that you spent hours doing?

A few people raise their hands and tell about ethical problems they had to solve. Elvira Portalupe tells about when the math teacher added her score wrong and she had to decide whether or not to tell him that she didn't really have an A. Elvira finishes by saying, "I decided that I didn't want a grade that I hadn't earned. I told him about his mistake and was much happier with my B+."

"Is she putting us on?" asks Arnold.

While somebody is telling about having to decide whether to keep taking piano lessons, Arnold raises his hand. It's the first time since he's been in class that he's had his hand in the air.

Ms. Karnisian passes over a couple of people and says, "Yes, Arnold?"

"Here's one for you," he says. "I never had no piano lessons, and I never had to give away my A grades, but this is something that really happened." It is funny to listen to him talk. He is using this tough-dumb voice, sort of like what you'd expect from a punch-drunk boxer. "Me an' this other guy was ridin' around in his car, an' he said why didn't we get a little somethin' to eat. I said that was okay by me, but what he meant was that we was gonna bust into this little grocery store. I was on the outside, an' he went through a window. While he was inside, he musta hit an alarm or somethin'. He tossed some stuff out the window to me—some cupcakes and fruit pies—

an' I started eatin' one. Right then the cops grabbed me. I had a whole armful of pies. What could I do?"

Arnold looks around the class for a minute and pulls himself around in his chair. "That ain't the question, though. You gotta have choices for an ethical question, right? An' the cops weren't givin' me no choices. But the guy inside, see, he heard somethin', an' he sneaked out the front door an' took off. So the cops had me, an' he was gone. They didn't care nothin' about me—I was only about twelve then—but the other guy was older, an' he'd been knockin' off places all around there. So they told me if I would tell them who was with me, they would let me go. Otherwise, they'd put me in juvie hall. Now that's an ethical question, right?"

"Sure," Ms. Karnisian says. She starts to move toward the blackboard.

"You know what I did? I was just twelve, see? I was just a kid. Dumb an' scared, see? I really believed 'em when they said they'd let me go if I'd rat on my buddy. I didn't want to go back to juvie. So you know what I did?" He waits for a minute. There is no noise at all in the room. "I told those cops . . . I told 'em . . . I told 'em they could kiss my . . . big toe."

The class breaks out laughing. Ms. Karnisian turns and writes on the blackboard, giving us our homework and our exercise book assignment. Arnold looks over at me and says, "Hey, Mickey Mouse, how do you spell 'confidential'?" I tell him. "Don't worry, man. I'm not writing my big secrets in my notebook. I just want to tell old Hatchetface how stupid I think it is to write something confidential and then have the teacher read it. But I didn't want to look like a dummy and spell it wrong."

"No problem," I say.

"Hey, Mickey Mouse," he says after a minute, "you believe that story I told about the store?"

"Sure," I say.

"It figures," he says. "You're dumb enough."

EIGHT

FROM THE NOTEBOOKS
Assignment: I had to choose between (list a value)
and (list another value).

JEFF GARRISON: I HAD TO CHOOSE BETWEEN DOING
my homework and breaking a girl's heart. This
girl asked me to come over last night, but I had
homework to do. It was a tough decision, but I
figured that she was more important than my
grades.

Jennifer Kirkpatrick: I had to choose between
honesty and freedom. My parents won't let me
go to a movie with a boy, so if I want to do it, I
have to get one of my friends to go with me to the
movies and meet the boy inside. (I only did this
once.)

Harry Beech: I had to choose between living with
my mother or my father. I didn't want to hurt
anybody's feelings, and I didn't know which one
I really wanted to live with. When my mother
decided to move to a new town, that settled it. I
chose my father. I'm glad I did. He's easy to get
along with.

Margaret Olson: I had to choose between fame
and Marshall Martin. Yesterday on my way home

from school, a big Cadillac stopped beside me, and a famous Hollywood director leaped out. He said I was exactly the person he had been looking for to star in his new movie. He said I could name my own terms. However, I told him that I was sorry, that I loved my school so much that I couldn't bear to miss a single day. He drove away crying.

Warren Cavendish: I can't think of any choices I have made that are worth writing about, but my mother made an interesting one last night. She and I had taken home a friend of hers who lives about ten miles from Hendley on a narrow winding road. On our way back to town, we came around a turn and saw a man in the middle of the road. He was waving his arms and yelling at us to stop. My mother slammed on the brakes to keep from hitting him, but then she steered around him and kept on going. As soon as we got back to town, she stopped at a phone booth and called the sheriff.

I thought she should have stopped for the man, but she said that she wasn't going to take a chance on a lonely road like that. She said that she was concerned about the man, which was why she called the sheriff, but that other things came first. I understand what she was saying, but I still think she should have stopped.

Arnold Norberry: (CONFIDENTIAL) Is this really confidential? Does that mean that no matter what I write, you won't say anything to anybody? That's what everybody says. What about this? I had to decide whether to stick around this nothing place or take off for somewhere else. I had a big fight with my mother last night, and I headed out. I found a car with the keys in it, and I started driving. But then I got to thinking how dumb it was to take off with no money and no plan. I would just get picked up and sent back to Juvie. And that's even worse than here. So I brought the car back and left it a few blocks from where I got it. Are you going to report me? It was a blue 1974 Pontiac.

NINE

TUESDAY, MAY 2

I'M LYING ON MY BED READING A BOOK. OR PRE-tending to, anyway. Mostly I'm listening to the music coming out of my sister's room and watching Arnold punch the numbers on my calculator. When I got it out to check my algebra homework, he wanted to try it. He'd never used one before. He started with little addition and subtraction problems, but pretty soon he was figuring out how many days he's been alive or how much money you'd have if you saved a nickel a day for a whole bunch of years.

It was my mother's idea to invite Arnold over. She said maybe we would get along better if we could spend some time by ourselves. She was right in a way—we've gotten along all right, just talking about school and things. But with Arnold I can't tell whether he's really listening. He seems kind of far away sometimes.

"Hey, Mickey," he says, "how much interest can you get if you put money in the bank?"

"I don't know. It depends."

He gives me this disgusted look. "Come on. What's the usual?"

"Five percent," I answer. I guess that's right.

He goes back to the calculator. "You know what?" he announces after a minute. "If you had a million dollars in the bank, you could spend a hundred and thirty-six dollars and ninety-eight cents a day, and you'd always have the million left."

"Great. All I need is the million to start with, and I've got it made.".

Arnold doesn't answer. He starts punching the calculator again.

A few minutes later my father calls that he's ready to take Arnold home. "That's all right," Arnold yells back. "I don't need a ride."

"I have to run into the library before it closes," my father calls. "You might as well ride that far anyway."

Arnold and I have gotten down the hall before I remember that I have a book to return. I trot back to my room and grab the book. Then, for some reason, I walk over and pick up the box that the calculator came in. It's empty.

"Hey, Arnold," I yell. "Come here a minute."

"Let's go, man. Your dad's waiting for us."

"Come back in here."

He stands in the hall and says, "Let's get on the move, man."

"Look," I tell him. "I know you took my calculator. If you want me to get my folks involved, it's all right with me."

"You're crazy," he says, but he comes back into the room and shuts the door. "I wouldn't take your calculator, man."

"Yes, you would. And I want it."

He looks at me with these sad eyes and shakes his head. "Come on, Mike. I wouldn't do that. You're about the only friend I got here in Hendley. You think I'd do something like that to you?"

For a minute I'm stuck. I want to believe him, especially when he's being decent to me for the first time. But I know better. "Give it to me," I say.

"Hey, man, I don't have it. It's around here somewhere. I know I set it down some place."

"You set it down in your pocket. Now give it back."

"You're gonna feel bad when it shows up. You're gonna wish you'd trusted me. Come on, man. Don't you trust me?"

"Come off it," I say. "How can I trust you when you just swiped my calculator?"

He turns away. "Forget it," he says in his old voice. "I'm sick of you anyway. If you can't even trust me, I don't need you. I've had it. Just don't bother me anymore, man."

"That suits me fine. But first I want the calculator."

He turns to face me, and for a minute I think we're going to fight. The whole idea of fighting scares me. Arnold isn't that much bigger than I am, but I've never been in a real fight. All I've had are little pushing things—one guy will start shoving the other, and both guys will say, "Watch it." I stand there and look at Arnold and wonder if this is going to be the real thing.

Then Arnold starts to laugh and takes the calculator from inside his shirt. It wasn't in his pocket after all—he had it stuffed in the waistband of his pants. I'm glad he brought it out. I never would have thought of looking there, and I don't know what I would have done if he had emptied his pockets to show he didn't have it. He hands me the calculator and taps my arm. "Don't take everything so serious, man. I was just putting you on."

I don't believe it, but it's a way to get the whole thing over with. "Right," I say.

He laughs as we walk down the hall. "Never can tell," he says, giving me a light punch on the arm. "Old Mickey Mouse turns out to be a tough old dude." And he laughs again.

I don't see anything funny.

We leave Arnold at the library. I have forgotten the book I was going to return, and it turns out that my dad doesn't need anything. He just figured that the library would give him an excuse to take Arnold most of the way home.

On the way back to our house, my dad says that there are some likable things about Arnold.

"Name one," I say.

"He's got pride, for one thing. He was willing to walk three miles rather than let us see where he lives."

"That's dumb. I don't care where he lives."

"Of course it's dumb. But anybody who cares that much about anything has possibilities."

I wonder what he would think of Arnold's possibilities if I told him about the calculator, but I keep my mouth closed.

TEN

FROM THE NOTEBOOKS
Assignment: Two things or people that make a contrast

JEFF GARRISON: IF YOU WANT A CONTRAST, PUT me next to Warren Cavendish. That's a contrast, no matter how you look at it. He's twice as big and twice as smart. I can run twice as fast, and I'm twice as ———. (I could say foxy here, but that would be bragging, so you look at the two of us and put in your own word.)

Harry Beech: On Channel 7 at three o'clock today is *It Came from Outer Space* (neat), and on Channel 4 is *The Edge of Night*, a soap opera (sickening). (CONFIDENTIAL) Arnold came over to my place the other night, and we sat around and watched TV and ate popcorn. He was all right. I guess he liked it because he came back again last night.

Jennifer Kirkpatrick: For lunch today Margaret had an egg salad sandwich, a chocolate eclair, an apple, and milk. I had some rye crackers and low-fat cheese. It isn't fair!!!

Margaret Olson: In the hallway during pass period, Mr. Vickers (the janitor) was talking to Mr.

Wagner (the math teacher). They are both about the same age and the same size, but one is a teacher and one is a janitor. The funny thing is, if you just met and talked to them, you would figure that Mr. Vickers was the teacher, not Mr. Wagner.

Arnold Norberry: Here's a contrast for you—me and the rest of the kids here. I might as well be on Mars. I heard a kid griping today because his father was too busy to take him to a baseball game. I felt like telling him that I wouldn't know my old man if I passed him on the street. Another guy asked me how much allowance I got. Do you know that some guys here get ten bucks a week just for spending money? There's your contrast.

Michael Parker: I sit in art class, and I have this really neat picture in my mind of an old barn by a pond, but when I try to put it on paper, the whole thing looks like some first grader's work. I know what it ought to look like—the picture is still there in my mind—but the picture on my paper is totally different. It's the kind of contrast that makes you want to cry.

Warren Cavendish: As I sit here trying to think of a contrast, I am watching Arnold (Joe Cool) Norberry leaning back in his seat. I don't know how he can even write in that position.

For a real contrast, you should have seen him at my place Friday night. He didn't know what to think at first, which is hardly surprising. With my father's collection of primitive masks, prayer rugs, Buddhas, etc., the whole apartment looks like an overcrowded museum. And I think my parents scared him, my mother the dentist and my father with the bushy beard and sandals.

After dinner when we started talking, though, Arnold began to relax. He and my mother discussed computers for a while. My father explained about collecting folklore and ended up recording two ghost stories that Arnold had heard in Juvenile Hall. The later it got, the more Arnold talked. It was long after midnight before we took him home.

For a few hours there, he forgot to be a hood. But by today, he's the same as before. When he came into class just now, he turned to me and said, "What's happening, Turkey Lurkey?"

ELEVEN

TUESDAY, MAY 9

TODAY EVERYBODY IS IN CLASS BEFORE THE BELL. We have a movie that will last two full periods, and even Harry is in his seat ahead of time. As the bell rings, somebody turns off the lights and the projector starts.

The movie is about this kid back in the old days, who spends a lot of time being cute and smart-alecky to everybody. I sit and wonder what Ms. Karnisian thought we were going to find to write about. Then about half an hour along, the big house where the kid lives catches on fire, and he's trapped up on the top floor. "Let the little turkey burn," Arnold says out loud.

The whole thing gets exciting. The kid is up in his room, yelling out the window, and the fire is crawling up the walls toward him. The kid's parents are outside the house, staring up at him. They can't do anything. This servant who has been the kid's best friend tries to go into the flaming house but can't make it. The kid keeps yelling for help.

Just then the chimes ring on the loudspeaker. Everybody groans. Ms. Karnisian shuts off the projector, and we sit and wait. The chimes sound again, and Mr. Bellows starts: "There have been some very dangerous practices occurring during the noon hour, and they must stop immediately. Anyone found with a peashooter or similar object will be suspended from school. There is a very real danger here of an eye injury. Besides, the peas left in the hallway are slippery and dangerous, as well as unsightly. So this is your warning. If anyone is found with a peashooter after today, that person will be suspended."

We wait for the chimes to ring again, but there is silence. Ms. Karnisian flips on the projector, and the flames are all over the screen. The boy is yelling for help, but we can't hear him because the sound is fouled up. A big flaming timber crashes down onto the dining room table, but we hear only the last part of the smashing. But then Mr. Bellows is speaking again, and the screen goes dark as the projector is switched off. " . . . that has been occurring at noon hour has to do with people who pass by our campus. Let me remind you that it is against the rules to speak to persons passing by on the street. You should treat that fence as if it were cement rather than wire. Ignore everything beyond the fence. There have been several reports of insults and foul language being used. . . ." And he goes on while we sit and twist in our chairs in the dark room.

When the message is finally over and the chimes ring, the movie comes on once again. The people out in the yard are staring at the burning house and moving their mouths. It's funny to see them waving their arms and throwing back their heads without any sound coming out. Then the speaker pops and blares, and people are screaming once again.

Meanwhile the flames are higher, and the boy's clothes are just starting to catch fire. He reaches down to slap the flames off one leg of his pants, and while he does this, the other leg catches fire. He keeps screaming, but it looks like nothing can be done. The servant says he has to try to save the boy, but people hold him back and tell him to be sensible. Just as he pushes everyone aside and races up the front steps of the burning house, the chimes ring again. The whole class groans, and Ms. Karnisian lets the film run for a minute before she turns it off. This only makes things worse because now the servant is in the middle of the flames and is crawling slowly up the stairs.

Mr. Bellows is saying, ". . . hope you will excuse the interruption, but you need to be reminded that all ninth-grade students who have not been measured for graduation robes should go to the library immediately after school today. . . ." There is more, but I don't listen. I've already heard this announcement today. Ms. Karnisian turns on the movie as soon as Mr. Bellows finishes. As the flames come back onto the screen, we hear the chimes.

At the end of class, the reel isn't quite finished. Except for the kids who have to catch buses, we stay afterward to watch the last part. The first reel ends with the people in the movie sort of mixed up. The servant is a big hero for saving the boy, but everybody feels funny around him because his face is horribly scarred.

As we come out of the room, Harry says, "Wow, that's neat. Sort of like *Phantom of the Opera.* That fire was the best part. I'll bet they had to burn down a real house to get those shots."

"And then Ding Dong Bellows comes chiming in," I say.

"There's no reason for that," Warren says. "Guys have been playing around that fence and yelling at old ladies on the sidewalk all year. It's been happening ever since the school was started. And that graduation junk was already announced fourth period."

"If it was me," Harry says, "I'd just let the movie run."

"Exactly," Jennifer says. "Why couldn't she just go ahead and show the movie?"

"I asked her that during the peashooting announcement," Margaret says. "She said she had to play by the rules."

"Maybe she has to play by the rules," Warren says, "but we don't. Tomorrow we're going to see the movie from start to finish. Or from middle to finish, I guess I should say." He looks at the rest of us. "At least we will if you'll help me."

"Help you do what?" I ask.

"Somebody has to make sure that Ms. Karnisian stays out of the room during pass period. The rest of it, I can take care of."

Everybody starts asking him questions, but this

is one of those times when Warren is ready to play *I've Got a Secret.* "You people just keep her out of the room. That's all you have to do. If you do your part, I'll do mine."

Would You Settle for Improbable?   74

To one of those times when Warren is asking, "Just like that—a secret?" You caught him looking out of the room, smiled, said, "I wish you'd come in, do your part, I'll do mine."

TWELVE

WEDNESDAY, MAY 10

I'M OUT OF MY FIFTH-PERIOD CLASS ON THE RUN. I don't have any part in what's going to happen, but I want to be around to see it. Jennifer says that she can keep Ms. Karnisian in the hall without anybody else's help, and Warren isn't even talking about what he's going to do. But I want to be there.

I miss most of the hall traffic and come through the door at 2:01. Instead of being in the hall as usual, Ms. Karnisian is setting up the projector at the back of the room. Warren is sitting at his desk, which he has moved out of the way of the projector. He points to Ms. Karnisian and shrugs his shoulders. I go down the aisle and stand beside her. "You want me to do that?" I say.

"I'll be your friend for life. Machines and I don't get along very well." She steps back, and I take over, moving the leader through each of the loops and sprockets. I feel sort of funny about the whole thing. I'm always running a projector for some teacher, so it's perfectly natural to be doing it here. But it's kind of dishonest at the same time.

While I'm fixing the take-up reel, Jennifer comes down the aisle and asks Ms. Karnisian if she can speak to her. Ms. Karnisian tells me to keep up the good work and turns to Jennifer.

"Could I talk to you outside?" Jennifer says, pulling at her hair. "It's sort of private."

"Sure," Ms. Karnisian says. "I'm supposed to be out there supervising anyway."

As soon as they're gone, Warren is out of his seat. "Watch the door," he whispers to the rest of us. He hurries to the side of the room and pulls a desk over to the wall, right beneath the loudspeaker. Moving as fast as I've ever seen him move, he climbs the desk and reaches up for the speaker. As he lifts it off the hook and turns it sideways, I notice the screwdriver and pliers in his hand. He holds the speaker against the wall with one hand and uses the other hand to try to get at something with the screwdriver.

Arnold walks into the room and heads down the aisle before he sees what's happening. He stops and grins. "Way to go, Lurkey," he whispers.

Warren doesn't seem to hear. He's still working on the back of the speaker. He goes at it from two different angles and then shakes his head. I keep looking from him to the clock and back. A minute has gone by, and the room is filling up quickly. Warren reaches underneath something, but the speaker shifts in his hand. He grabs it with both hands, and the screwdriver clatters to the floor. Two or three guys dive for it. "Never mind," Warren says. He reaches up with the pliers and snips something. Then he places the speaker back onto the hook once more.

"Here she comes," somebody whispers. Warren

leaps off the desk and lands in the aisle, but his feet get tangled. He crashes against another desk and sprawls on the floor. Ms. Karnisian steps into the room and then rushes toward him.

Warren gets to his feet quickly. "It's all right," he says. "I'm not hurt. No thanks to somebody. You'd think that people in the ninth grade would be too old for kindergarten tricks. Reach out and trip somebody. How hilarious." He brushes himself off, then bends over, pretending to fix his pants leg while he stuffs the pliers into his sock.

Ms. Karnisian looks around as if she isn't sure whether to follow up on the tripping business, but the bell rings as Warren heads for his desk. "Go ahead and start the film, Michael," she says. I flip the switch while somebody turns out the lights. Then I settle back to watch the movie without any interruptions.

The movie ends in a strange kind of way, and I'm still trying to decide whether or not I like it when the door opens. The lights go on in the room, and Mr. Bellows is standing there. He calls Ms. Karnisian into the hall for a minute. I look over at Warren, but he's staring straight at the floor. Mr. Bellows comes back into the room first, with Ms. Karnisian two steps behind him. He walks over to the loudspeaker, asks a girl to get up from her desk, and moves the desk right under the speaker, just the way Warren did.

Mr. Bellows takes longer to get the speaker off the hook than Warren did, and then he stares into the back of it. "Look at this," he says to Ms.

Karnisian, who is steadying the desk. "This wire has been cut."

"Could it have broken?" she asks quietly.

"Look at it," he says. "See how the ends look? It's been cut all right."

I glance over at Warren and see him trying to transfer the pliers into his waistband. Scared as I am, I can't help thinking that Warren remembers what I told him about Arnold and the calculator. Ms. Karnisian looks at Jennifer and then at me. I try to look at her forehead so that I can keep looking her way without catching her eyes. I feel my face getting hot.

Mr. Bellows walks to the front of the room and says, "Ladies and gentlemen, a serious act of vandalism has taken place in this classroom, and we are going to get to the bottom of it. Someone in here cut the wire to the loudspeaker. If there had been a real emergency, that cut wire might have cost lives. Fortunately there was not an emergency. I was merely attempting to page this room and received no response. So, in another sense, we are fortunate. We have found the cut wire before any harm was done, and we know that someone here is the guilty party. Ms. Karnisian tells me that the loudspeaker was functioning during fifth period. So someone here is responsible. And nobody is going to leave this room until I know the truth."

Nobody says a word. Warren has managed to get the pliers into his waistband and to cover them with his shirt, but his hands are shaking. I think for a minute that I ought to stand up and confess, but that would mean telling on everybody else. Besides, as I think about it some more, the whole idea scares me silly.

"I'm in no hurry," Mr. Bellows says. "Of course, the buses will be leaving soon, and some of you may be forced to make other arrangements to get home. But there is a valuable lesson here. When the safety of the entire student body is at stake, it is no time for misguided notions about loyalty. It is important for all concerned that we get at the truth. Now, instead of just sitting here, why don't we see if anyone has something he or she would like to say? I have the same question to ask of each of you: Do you know anything about how the wire on the loudspeaker was cut? I will ask that question of each of you." He turns to Mildred Wainwright, this little mousy girl who sits by the door. "What about you? Do you know anything about this?"

Mildred turns a reddish purple and puts her head down. "No," she says in a tiny voice. If I didn't know better, I would figure that she was the guilty one. But I know that she wasn't in class yesterday and that she came in today after Warren hit the floor. So there she is, possibly the only totally innocent person in the room, and she looks ready to confess.

Mr. Bellows takes a step or two toward her desk. "Are you sure?"

Mildred nods her head and then puts it down on her desk. She will not look up at Mr. Bellows, although he keeps staring at her.

He finally gives up and goes down the row. Everybody says "No" except Jeff Garrison, who sits up straight in his chair and states, "I have no information whatsoever." A few people snicker, but Mr. Bellows stares them down.

Sitting in the last seat in the row is Jennifer. Usually that seat is empty, but Jennifer has had to move there because of the projector. I glance over at her, and I can see her lower lip trembling.

"You," Mr. Bellows says, "the girl in the last seat, do you know anything about it?" Jennifer just sits and stares at him, her whole lower jaw shaking. She reaches up and pushes her hair away from her face. "Well, do you?"

There isn't a sound in the room. Then the bell rings, and the whole class jumps. Afterwards there is some nervous laughter, and Mr. Bellows even smiles. "As I said, we'll stay here until we are finished." He looks at Ms. Karnisian, then turns back to Jennifer. I want to do something, but I can't figure what to do. Mr. Bellows clears his throat. "I am waiting for an answer." I can't look at Jennifer any longer. As Mr. Bellows heads toward her desk, he says, "I would like your answer right now."

Just then Arnold stands up. "Mr. Bellows," he says, "they're just trying to keep from telling on me. I was the one who did it."

Mr. Bellows looks a little surprised, and I think for a minute that he's angry because things didn't work out the way he expected. "You did, did you?"

"Yessir," Arnold says. "It was kind of an accident, but I did it. I would have said so before, but I'm new here, and didn't know what you'd do." While he talks, he keeps looking at Mr. Bellows, then down at the floor, then back at Mr. Bellows again.

Mr. Bellows watches him for a minute, as if he's trying to guess his weight or something. "And just how did you cut that wire?"

"With this," Arnold says. He reaches into his pocket and brings out a long thin pocketknife.

"The rest of you may go," Mr. Bellows says. "Those of you who ride buses, get a move on. You still have time to make it." The room empties much faster than it does for any fire drill.

I'm thinking about confessing along with Arnold, but I can't seem to find the courage to do it. Instead, I go over and start to take care of the projector. I thread the film for rewinding and act like I have no interest in what's going on in the front of the room. I don't know if Mr. Bellows looks at me or not, because I keep my eyes on the projector.

"I guess I shoulda told you right away," Arnold says. "I was scared, though."

"Now tell me, young man—what's your name?"

"Arnold, sir. Arnold Norberry."

"Now tell me, Arnold. Just how did you accidentally happen to be up there eight feet in the air in the first place?"

"I was messing with the speaker," Arnold says. Mr. Bellows grunts. "When I said it was an accident, I didn't mean that I didn't do anything wrong. I did. I was up there messing with the speaker."

"What were you doing?"

"The whole thing was dumb. There's this girl that sits in front of me. I sit over there in the next-to-last row. This girl, she's always complaining because she can't hear the announcements when they come on. And I always have to tell her what you said. So I thought I'd fix her. I thought I'd get up there and turn up the volume. I wanted it to blast her out of her seat. It was a stupid idea."

"It certainly was," Mr. Bellows says, but he doesn't sound as angry as he did before.

"Well, see, I got up there while Ms. Karnisian was out of the room, but I couldn't figure out which one was the volume. There was this one screw that I figured had to be the one, and I got out my knife and was using it to turn the screw. Then somebody yelled, 'Here she comes,' and I jumped and almost dropped the speaker. When I was grabbing for it, I cut that wire. She wasn't coming. They were just trying to scare me. The wire wasn't cut all the way through. I bent it a little to see if it was all right, and it snapped in two. I didn't know what to do. I tried to put the ends together so they would stay, and then I put the speaker back. I was hoping nobody would find out about it. The whole thing was stupid."

"That's for sure," Mr. Bellows says.

"Yessir," Arnold says quietly.

"Well, Arnold. Your name was Arnold, wasn't it?"

"Yessir. Arnold Norberry."

"I'll take your knife now, Arnold."

"Yessir."

"At the end of the year, you can come to the

office and get it. That is, if you've behaved yourself in the meantime."

"I will, sir."

"I hope so. Now, Arnold, the question is what to do with you. You ought to be suspended. You know that, don't you?"

"Yessir."

"How long have you been here at Marshall Martin?"

"This is just my third week."

"Do you like it here?"

"Yessir, I do."

"Well, Arnold, if you like it here, you'd better not let this sort of thing happen again. If it does, you'll be looking for a new school. Do you understand?"

"Yessir."

"I'm going to let you go this time, but don't start thinking I'm easy. I'm giving you a second chance, but you'll never get a third."

"Thank you, sir," Arnold says.

"I'm giving you a break," Mr. Bellows says. "Make the most of it." He turns to Ms. Karnisian. "I'll have Mr. Vickers fix that speaker right away." He walks out the door and closes it behind him.

Arnold goes back to his desk, grabs up his books, and heads for the door like somebody with a bus to catch.

"That's far enough," Ms. Karnisian says. Arnold stops and grins at her, but I notice that he backs up against the wall. "Do you want me to clap for your performance?"

Arnold looks down at the floor. I put the film in

the can and start gathering up the electric cord, trying to be as quiet and busy as I can.

"I don't know, Arnold," she says. "That was a new one for me. What should I have done? I knew perfectly well that you were lying the whole time. Should I have stepped in and called you a liar in front of Mr. Bellows?"

"But I . . ."

"Save it, sir," she says. "What a pile of garbage that was. You've been out of the hall too long, I guess. You're losing your touch. You were unscrewing something, and you got scared and jumped back and, gee whiz, cut the wire. Come on, Arnold. You can do better than that."

"I'm sorry," Arnold says.

"Don't start that stuff with me. You want to start calling me ma'am too? I told you before, saying you're sorry afterward doesn't change anything. But you tell me, Arnold. Here's your ethical problem for the day—should I have called you a liar while Mr. Bellows was here?"

"I don't know," Arnold mutters. "I thought you were going to. I wouldn't have blamed you if you did."

"I came close to it, I'll tell you that. You better be glad Mr. Bellows is a decent man. He gave you as good a break as you're ever going to get. You remember that." She walks up closer to him, and I think for a minute that she's going to hit him. But she reaches out and messes up his hair. "Get out of here. I don't know what's going on, and I don't want to know. You know what I was saying to myself while I stood there and listened to you telling fairy tales? I was saying, 'He'd better have a good reason for doing this.' And I hope you did, and I don't want to know what it was. Now go on."

"Right," Arnold says. "See you later." He goes out the door in a hurry.

I've been standing at the back of the room, waiting for her to finish. Now I pick up my books and start up the aisle. I keep expecting her to say something to me, but she doesn't. By the time my hand hits the doorknob, I'm thanking my lucky stars to be getting out of there. But then I just can't go on out the door. I turn around and watch Ms. Karnisian straighten some shelves.

"Ms. Karnisian?"

"Yes, Michael?"

"I was in on it."

She looks at me and laughs. "You'll never make a poker player, Michael. It was all over your face."

"It won't happen again."

"Once is enough for me."

"And, Ms. Karnisian," I say as I start out the door, "the whole thing was stupid, but I think that Arnold had a good reason for what he did." I leave before she can say anything.

Arnold is waiting for me in the hall. He grins and comes dancing toward me. "You got us all off," I say.

"No big thing, man."

"It was to me. You really handled that neat."

"There's a good lesson for you, Mickey. When you gotta spill the beans, don't ever confess to what they think you did. When they're mad about one thing, they'll let almost anything else go by."

"I'm not going to have to confess to anything," I say, "because I'm not going to do anything. That was one of the roughest afternoons I ever spent."

"Come on, man. That was no big thing."

"Maybe not to you. Anyway, thanks for doing what you did. You were really something."

Arnold grins and looks away. Then he turns back and says. "You are becoming singularly unamusing." He laughs and taps me on the arm. "You didn't think I could talk like that, did you?"

THIRTEEN

FROM ARNOLD NORBERRY'S POCKETS

Dear Arnold,

I don't know how to thank you. I was so scared. I just couldn't say anything to Mr. Bellows. I knew that Ms. Karnisian would see right through the whole thing. Thank you, Arnold. That was one of the nicest things anybody ever did for me.

Jennifer

Esteemed Arnold:

You have my undying gratitude for your sacrificial action. Although one might question your judgment, your intentions and your bravery are irreproachable. As I am indebted to you for my freedom, I remain your eternally grateful and humble servant.

Warren Cavendish, Esquire

RECEIPT FOR CONFISCATED PROPERTY

This is to certify that a(n)   *pocketknife*
_____
(description of article)

has been confiscated from   *Arnold Norberry*   on
_____
(name of student)

5/10/1978 .
_____
(date)

This property ( ) will be destroyed.

( ) will be returned on _____.

( ) will be returned after a parent conference.

(X) will be returned on *6/14/1978* under these conditions:

No disciplinary problems between now and the end of school.
_____

All property that is not reclaimed will be donated to charity or destroyed.

CLIFFORD BELLOWS, PRINCIPAL

FOURTEEN

SATURDAY, MAY 13

ON SATURDAY MY SISTER HAS SOME FRIENDS OVER, so I decide to ride my bicycle over to Arnold's. I know about where he lives, although I've never been there. It's a warm day, and I feel good riding along. I'm glad to be heading for Arnold's. He's been to my house several times, and he's told me that I should come by his place some time, but I've been sort of afraid. The area where he lives is in what people call "the rough part of town" or "the Hendley slum," but I'm going anyway. I want to show Arnold that I don't care where he lives.

Riding along Vincent Avenue, next to the railroad tracks, I start feeling less sure of myself. The houses along there are all kind of pushed together, and there are trashed-out cars on the streets and in people's yards. A lot of people are sitting around out in front of their houses. For some reason this bothers me. Where we live, the only time you'll see somebody in the front yard is when they're mowing the lawn or trimming the hedge or something.

Some young kids are playing football in the street, and they don't move when a car comes along. They walk to the side slowly, after the car has almost stopped. Then they crowd up to the car as it goes by. They don't pay much attention to me as I sort of dodge my way through them, except that one little boy—about six years old—yells a bunch of dirty names at me.

I turn on Collins Street, which is where Arnold lives, and ride past a small grocery store called the Good Buy Market. Two men are sitting on the sidewalk in front of the market, drinking out of bottles wrapped in paper bags. There are old sacks and beer cans all over the street, and I have to weave around to keep from running over any of the trash. One of the men yells at me, but I keep on riding like I don't hear him.

I have trouble finding Arnold's place because there aren't any numbers on the houses. Arnold has said that he lives on the corner of Collins and Taylor, and his address—996 Collins—means that he's on the right hand side of the street. But the only place 996 can be is a big, old-fashioned house with a couple of stories and fancy little windows up under the roof. This has to be the place, but I know that Arnold and his mother wouldn't live in a house this big.

Six wooden steps lead up to the front door. The middle of each step is all worn down, sort of like a trail across a field. I walk up the steps and knock on the door. Nothing happens. After knocking twice more, I go back to my bicycle. I pretend there's something wrong with my gearshift, and I bend over and fiddle with it. I want to wait around a few minutes in case Arnold comes back, but I don't want to look like I'm just hanging around.

While I'm bent over my bike, a woman comes from the store with a sack of groceries. She goes up the steps, shoves open the front door, and walks inside. The door doesn't shut all the way, so I go back up the steps and look in. When I do, I feel really dumb. The place isn't a house at all. The front door just leads to a hallway and then some stairs. Every door off the hall is a different apartment. Some of the doors have metal numbers on them, and some have places where the numbers used to be a long time ago.

I'm stuck, though. I don't know which apartment is Arnold's, and I don't feel like knocking on some stranger's door and asking. I'm just standing there, half in and half out the door, when somebody grabs me by the shoulder. I look around and see this big black woman. She must weigh three hundred pounds, and I can't figure how she could come up behind me without my hearing her. She has a solid handful of my shirt and shoulder, and she seems to be trying to make her fingers touch her thumb through my skin. "What you up to, boy?"

"A friend of mine lives here," I say.

"You got no call to be nosin' round here." She doesn't ease up on my shoulder at all.

"His name is Arnold Norberry. He lives here."

"Him? That trash?" She gives me a shove without letting go of me. "You better watch yourself.

You let me catch you hangin' round my place again, I'll chop you up into dogmeat."

"I just didn't know which one is his apartment, ma'am," I say. "I've never been here before, and I don't know which one is his."

"You want to find that trash, just use your nose. You can tell by the smell." She lets out this strange-sounding laugh and shoves me aside. I'm glad to get my shoulder back. After she makes it through the doorway, she turns back to me. I move down the steps far enough to be sure that I'm out of reach. "Just don't let me catch you hangin' round," she says. " 'Cause if you do, you gonna be dogmeat. Now ain't that sweet." She lets out the same kind of laugh again and walks down the hallway.

I keep waiting for somebody else to show up, but nobody does. I can hear a TV set going inside, so I decide to knock on that door and ask about Arnold. The hallway smells funny, sort of like a stuffy kitchen and a wet basement at the same time. I walk down the hall and tap on the door where I hear the TV.

"Who is it?" somebody yells from inside.

"I'm looking for Arnold," I say.

"Who is it?"

"I'm looking for Arnold."

"Ain't no Art here."

I've had enough. I turn around and head for the door. But then Arnold yells at me from the top of the stairway. "Hey, Mickey, what's happening?"

I'm really glad to see him. He moves down the

long staircase, half dancing, the way he does when
everything is all right. It's good to have something
be normal. "I was just riding around," I tell him.
It's a dumb thing to say. You don't just happen to
ride around and come to Collins Street.

We walk through the front door and start down
the steps. There are two boys standing by my bike.
"Touch it, and we'll send you home in a box,"
Arnold yells.

"You and what army?" one of them yells back,
but they move away.

Arnold and I sit on the steps and talk a little.
From where I'm sitting, I can see maybe twenty
people sitting out on the steps of their houses.

After a while Arnold asks me if I want a Coke.
I expect to go back into the house, but we go down
the street to the store. It's funny walking along
the sidewalk with Arnold. He'll step around a
wino and not even seem to see him. Two or three
people say hello to Arnold, but the rest drift by us
like we're invisible.

Just as we reach the entrance to the store, I feel
somebody grab my shoulder. I immediately think
of the black woman and yank away. I turn to see
an old man standing there. He has jerked back
like he thinks I'm going to hit him. He's wearing
a blue suit, but he must have had it on for weeks.
He smiles at me, and only a few brown teeth
show in his mouth. "Hey, young feller," he says,
"how 'bout givin' a guy a break? Gimme a quarter,
huh? How 'bout it? How 'bout some change?"

I just stand there, not quite sure what to do.

Arnold steps back out of the door. "Shove off," he tells the old man. "Come on, Mickey."

When we come out of the store with our drinks, the old man is still standing by the door. He looks away as Arnold goes by, but he says to me, "It wouldn't hurt you none. You wouldn't miss it."

We sit down on the steps at Arnold's place, and he tosses me a bag of peanuts and opens one for himself. I don't know where the peanuts came from, whether he had them before or whether he took them in the store. Arnold finishes his Coke and tosses the can off to the side. I don't know what to do with mine, so I leave it sitting on the steps. Which is dumb. At least where Arnold threw his, nobody's going to trip over it. But I don't feel right about tossing my can on the ground that way.

It gets harder and harder for me to think of something to say, but luckily Arnold feels like talking. He's telling me about this kid named Prutch who kept trying to escape from juvenile hall. While he talks, this woman comes walking up to the stairs where we're sitting. She's moving very carefully, like she's walking on ice or something. I wouldn't pay much attention to her except that her hair is pink. Not blond with a little touch of something. Real pink—like a rabbit's nose. Her hair doesn't match the rest of her at all. Her face is pale and tired looking, with those lines on the sides of the eyes that make faces look squinched up.

"Who's your friend, Arnold?" the woman says.

She's right next to the steps, but she talks as if we're halfway down the block.

"This is Mike," Arnold says. He gets up and walks over by the bike.

"How do you do, Mike?" She reaches out for my hand. Once she has it, she keeps squeezing it. "I'm always happy to meet Arnold's friends."

I say hello and try to get back my hand, but she holds on.

"Do you live around here, Mike?" She shouts at me.

"No," I say very quietly, hoping she'll get the idea. "I was just riding by on my bike." I pull my hand out of hers, and for a second I think she's going to fall. She manages to get her balance though.

"Do you go to Arnold's school?" she asks in the same loud voice.

"Let's go inside," Arnold says.

"That would be nice," the woman says, but she doesn't move.

"You go ahead and go in," he says. "We'll be right there."

The woman keeps standing in the same place, except that she moves back and forth a little, shifting her weight from one foot to the other. "I'm always happy to meet Arnold's friends," she says, even louder than before.

"Hey, Ma," Arnold says, "go on inside, okay?"

Only when he says this do I know for sure that this woman is his mother. I guess I knew it before, but it hadn't really sunk in.

"I'll go inside when I'm good and ready," she yells at him.

From one of the upstairs windows somebody shouts, "Will you shut up down there?"

Arnold comes over and takes his mother's arm. "Let's go inside, Ma."

All of a sudden she's crying. "I don't know why people have to be the way they are. There's no excuse at all." She wipes her eyes with her sleeve and looks at me. "I'm always happy to meet Arnold's friends."

"Ma, let's move it."

"I haven't finished speaking with your friend," she yells.

"Yes, you have," he says. He begins to move her up the steps, partly pulling her and partly carrying her. He seems to know exactly how to move her, as if he's had plenty of practice.

"Don't you treat me like this in front of your friend," she shouts. "I will not have you treat me this way."

"Just come on, will ya?" Arnold says. He steps through the front door and guides her past him.

Just then she turns and slaps him hard across the face. Except for movies, I've never seen anybody slap anybody else that way. "Don't you treat me this way. I won't allow it."

Somebody yells, "Hold it down out there," from behind one of the doors.

"Aah, stick it in your ear," Arnold yells back. He grabs both of his mother's arms and pulls her down the hall and up the stairs. She fights back at first, but then she just follows along.

I don't know what to do. I want to get on my bike and ride home and never come back. But I don't know what I'd say to Arnold the next time I saw him. So I sit and wait.

He comes back sooner than I expect. "No big thing, man," he says as he sits down on the steps. "She gets like that sometimes when she's had a few." Then he goes on telling me about how Prutch tried to sneak a hacksaw into juvenile hall. He doesn't mention his mother again, and I don't either.

After a while I get on my bike and ride home. But I can't get the whole thing straight in my mind. I can't see why Arnold has to live in a place like that. Why should he have to have winos on his sidewalks? And why do I feel so funny down on Collins Street? I don't think I'm better than anybody else, but I feel out of place down there.

What bothers me most is that I don't think Arnold realized how weird it was for me. I hope he didn't anyway. He's so used to the way things are there that he doesn't seem to notice them. But why should a guy have to get to the point where it's normal to have his mother drunk and his neighbors yelling at him?

I keep thinking that it isn't fair. And that reminds me of Ms. Karnisian, who is always saying, "Nobody ever said life is fair." But that doesn't solve anything.

By the time I get home, I am very, very tired.

FIFTEEN

FROM THE NOTEBOOKS
Assignment: Describe something that turned out differently than you expected it to.

JEFF GARRISON: YESTERDAY I GOT INTO A FIGHT in metal shop with a kid named Denny Wittner. I was just walking by him, and he laid one on my ear. I gave him some back with interest. Mr. Aiken took us both to Mr. Bellows's office. Mr. Bellows took Denny inside first, and I had to sit out in front and wait. The longer I sat there, the more nervous I got.

But when Mr. Bellows got me into his office, he wasn't mean at all. He told me that Denny was having bad problems and thought everybody was laughing at him. Then he talked about how things were when he was in school. He had some coffee and gave me a doughnut to eat. So it wasn't what I expected. I figured he was going to suspend me, and he ended up giving me a doughnut and talking about things in the old days.

Jennifer Kirkpatrick: Last week when my mother and father were out of town, I stayed with my cousin, who is a sophomore in high school. On Saturday she asked me if I wanted to go to Disco-Teen, and I was dying to go. I've been hearing about the place since it opened, but my parents won't let me go. I thought it would be really neat, with all the high school kids there and everything.

It was all right at first. There are all these wild posters and flashing lights. But once you got used to the place, it was just like one of the Marshall Martin dances. The record would start, and just a few kids would dance. The girls stood around in circles and talked, and most of the boys were over playing the pinball machines. I only danced two times the whole night, and one of them was with this creepy guy named Ralph, who kept making dumb noises the whole time we danced.

Harry Beech: When my mother told me that she and my father were getting a divorce, I didn't think I could stand it. The whole thing scared me, and when I told people about it, they all said how sorry they were. I was really rotten to both my mother and dad, telling them that I hated them for doing it.

The divorce didn't turn out the way I thought it would, though. I live with my dad most of the time, and we get along good. I call my mother on the phone and go see her sometimes. Things are different than they were before, but they aren't the way I thought they would be.

In some ways I still wish I lived with both my parents in the old house we had before, but in other ways I don't. It's hard to decide.

Margaret Olson: (This is kind of dumb, but I can't think of anything else to write about.) Last year I was in a car pool with some ninth-grade girls. All they could talk about last spring was graduation and the dance afterwards. I couldn't believe it. It seemed so stupid to be talking in April about what shoes you were going to wear in June. I made up my mind right then that I was going to skip the whole thing. I even asked my mother if graduation was required, and she said it wasn't. So I decided that I was going to miss the whole foolish business.

But now that I'm in the ninth grade, things seem different. I'm going to take part in graduation, and I'm sort of looking forward to it. I'm not about to get hysterical over the pink dress that I picked out, but it's a nice dress. I still haven't decided whether to go to the dance afterward, but I don't think that everybody who goes to the dance has oatmeal for brains, which is the way I felt last year. I guess things change when you're the one involved.

Arnold Norberry: This school isn't what I thought it would be. If some of the guys at the hall heard about me, they wouldn't believe it. On the science test we just got back, I got the second highest grade in the class. What do you think about that? Not too bad for a Juvie Hall dummy, is it?

Don't get any ideas. I'm still the same guy. But some of the stuff here is interesting—not like the baby stuff they gave us at the hall. A lot of the teachers here are the same old story, but there are a couple, like Mr. Fernandez, who treat kids like they have some brains.

SIXTEEN

THURSDAY, MAY 18

ALL THIS WEEK PEOPLE HAVE BEEN TALKING about graduation, even ones like Warren, who used to say that it was the silliest waste of time ever concocted. Now that Warren has been selected to give a speech, he has decided that it isn't so bad. The girls keep talking about their dresses, although I can't see why the dresses matter. We're all wearing robes anyway.

I'm heading into English class when Arnold catches up with me. "Hey, Mickey," he says, "hold on a second." He pulls me off to one side and says, "Listen, man, I want to ask you something, and I don't want you to make a big deal out of it. I don't care if you think it's dumb, but I don't want you to laugh."

"I'll try," I say. "But you'd better hurry. We have less than a minute before the bell."

"So what, man? So you come in after the bell rings—what's the big deal?" He looks around, making sure that nobody is standing too close. Then he says in this voice that is just above a whisper, "Listen, see, you know this graduation? What does somebody have to do to graduate?"

I start to say something smart like, "Breathe often enough to show you're still alive," but then I realize that it might not be that easy for Arnold, with him changing schools and being in juvenile hall. "I'm not too sure," I say. "I guess I could find out."

"No big thing," he whispers. "I was just kind of wondering. I prob'ly can't do it or anything, but I was just wondering. If you could go ahead and find out, I wouldn't mind knowing. You know what I mean."

So I go into the room and write a quick note to Ms. Karnisian, saying that Arnold wants to know whether he can graduate. While we are writing in our notebooks about a possession that is important to us, she puts a note on my desk saying that she will check on it.

As soon as class is over and the room starts to clear, Arnold is standing beside my desk. "What did she say, Mickey?"

"Why don't you just ask her yourself?"

"Come on, Mickey. Don't be a nerd, huh? What did she say?"

"She said she didn't know. She'll have to find out."

Arnold lets out a long breath. "No big thing. They prob'ly won't let me, me just getting here a little while ago."

"Well, Ms. Karnisian will check on it anyway."

"She said she would, huh?"

"Right."

"It's prob'ly a waste of time. They prob'ly won't let me. But even if they decide I can, I don't have a robe ordered. And I don't think you can do it if you don't have a robe. You wouldn't want to, even if you could. I mean, that would look stupid—to be the only one there without a robe on. It's prob'ly too late to order robes, isn't it?"

"How would I know?"

"Maybe you could ask her. You know, what happens if a person can graduate, but they don't have a robe ordered?"

By this time there's nobody else in the room except Ms. Karnisian and Elvira Portalupe. "All right," I say, "I'll ask her if you want me to."

"Might as well," he says. "No big thing. I was just kind of wondering. You know what I mean."

He's out of the room like a shot, and I'm left there listening to Ms. Karnisian explain to Elvira why too many adjectives weaken a paper. When Elvira has her question answered, she glares at me and walks out. She obviously figures I'm invading her territory.

Ms. Karnisian looks at me and smiles. She pulls her hair away from her face with both hands. "So he wants to graduate, does he?"

"Right," I say. "But now he wants to know what happens if he doesn't have a robe ordered."

She puts her face in her hands and laughs. First it's a kind of halfway laugh, but then she lets go and roars. "A robe? A robe? He's missed half the days of school since he was nine years old, and he's worried about a robe?" She suddenly stops laughing. "I'm not laughing at him, Michael. Actually I am, but not in the way you think. All right. I'll see what I can find out. And if there's any chance of his graduating, I'll make sure he has a robe, if I have to sew it myself. Where is he now? Standing out in the hall?"

"I don't know."

"Well, tell him I'll look into everything as soon as I can." She shakes her head and starts to smile.

"Thank you," I say.

"Michael, I wish he didn't have his hopes set on this. I don't think his chances of graduating are very good. I have no idea what his transcript looks like, but I can imagine. But we won't play down the importance of it. It matters to him, and if he can't graduate, he's going to be disappointed and unhappy. And there's no use pretending otherwise."

As I come out the door, Arnold is leaning against the wall. "Well, what did she say?"

"I already told you. She said she'd check."

"Sometimes you just try to be dumb. You know that? I mean about the robe. What did she say about the robe?"

"She said if there was any chance of you graduating, she would make sure you had a robe."

Arnold starts to grin. "All *right*," he says. He walks along with me for a minute, then says, "No big thing, you know."

"Right," I say.

"And don't go telling anybody, okay? Just keep it quiet."

I keep thinking all afternoon about Arnold wanting to graduate from Marshall Martin. It's hard to figure. I'm going to wear my robe and get my diploma, and I know that my parents will be there. So will my sister, if she doesn't have a date or something. But it's just a junior high school graduation. Arnold is right when he says, "No big thing," but he doesn't believe it the way I do.

SEVENTEEN

FROM THE NOTEBOOKS
Assignment: Describe a possession that is important to you. Explain why it is important.

ELVIRA PORTALUPE: MY PRIZE POSSESSION IS A gold plaque that was given to me for being the Outstanding Campfire Girl in the Twelfth District. It is only a plaque, but it symbolizes to me all of the hours I spent on projects and all the wonderful people I met during my years as a Campfire Girl. . . .

Jeff Garrison: I don't have many possessions, but one that is important to me is the dollar in my pocket. Just as soon as this class is over, I am going downtown to the A&W and get a chocolate shake. Then I will take my change and go over to the bowling alley and play pinball. The way I feel today, I bet I can play all afternoon on one quarter.

Margaret Olson: A possession that is important to me is my heart. It is not particularly beautiful. In fact, it is red and kind of slimy with all sorts of arteries and veins hooked up to it. And it doesn't do much except expand and contract. But I am fond of it anyway. If it was not there doing its job, I would not be here doing mine.

Arnold Norberry: One thing I have that I like is a little silver cup that says OUR HERO on it. A girl here gave it to me, and it's neat. You can get them at the Rexall Drug Store for about a buck, but this one is special because she gave it to me.

Warren Cavendish: In my closet at home I have a brand new basketball. Last year my father brought it home and gave it to me. I asked him why he got me a ball when he knew that I didn't like sports. He said that he didn't like sports either, but that he figured I ought to have a choice. So I put the ball in my closet and never used it. I think, though, that my father had a good idea. What he was trying to say to me was that I could do whatever I wanted, that he wouldn't try to make me be the way he is. Or maybe he just felt like buying a ball. You can't always tell about him. Anyway, I like the ball, even if I never use it.

Michael Parker: This is hard to write about. I have lots of possessions, but I can't think of any that are especially important to me. I have a whole set of shelves in my room crammed full of puzzles and models and books and everything from yo-yos to paint brushes. Somehow it doesn't seem right. I don't need—I never did need—half the stuff I have. I would have been just as happy with half as much. Or a quarter.

Actually, that's not true. At Christmas time I was always hunting around the tree to see if there wasn't just one more package with my name on it. I did like getting all those things, even if I didn't need them. But now that I have them, I wouldn't miss them if they were taken away.

Why should I have so much and other people have nothing? When Arnold comes over to my house, he likes to come into my room and mess with the stuff that I have. I always feel funny when he does. Why couldn't he have some of the things? I'm sort of mixed up here. I'm just getting started, and I'm not sure where I'm going, and I'm out of time anyway.

EIGHTEEN

FRIDAY, MAY 19

As I come into English class, Arnold is sitting on my desk. "I haven't heard anything yet," I say. "I just got here, and she was talking to somebody out in the hall."

"What're you talking about, man?" Arnold says.

I look around to be sure nobody is listening. "You know—graduation."

"Come on, Mickey. You think I was waiting here for that? You're out of your mind." He moves over to his seat, and I notice that he doesn't have anything else he wants to ask me.

When class is over Ms. Karnisian asks to see Arnold and me. Arnold gets this half-sick smile on his face and makes a throat-cutting motion for the people around him. He and I sit at our desks until the rest of the students file out of the room, including those who are hanging back to see if they can find out what we've done. Once the door is closed, we move up to the front of the room.

Ms. Karnisian comes around and sits on her desk. "Arnold," she says, "I've done some checking. First, I want you to know that I'm very pleased. You're doing very well here at Marshall Martin.

Your teachers have only good things to say about you, especially Mr. Fernandez. He says you have a very quick mind."

"But I can't graduate, right?" Arnold says. The way he says it, you would think that Ms. Karnisian is the one to blame.

"Probably not."

Arnold grabs up his books and heads for the door. "Thanks for nothin'," he says.

"What's your hurry?" Ms. Karnisian says. "You might as well stick around and hear the whole thing."

Arnold reaches for the doorknob. "Yeah. Well, what difference does it make?"

Her voice comes across harder than I've ever heard it. "I don't know, buddy. But I didn't ask for help—you did. And it took me about five hours to find out what I did. I figure you can spare five minutes to hear it."

Arnold leans up against the doorframe with that show-me-something slouch of his. "So?"

"You remember Miss Evans, Arnold? From Oak Crest Junior High?"

"That old bag. What about her?"

"Do you remember what class you took from her?"

"I don't know. Social studies, civics? I don't know what they call it."

"Do you remember the Constitution test at the end of the year? The one they said you had to pass?"

"I guess so."

"You didn't pass it. In fact, I spoke to Miss

Evans this morning. Do you remember what you did on that test?" Arnold shrugs. "According to her, you just marked all the questions false and turned in your paper. Then when you failed the test, you told her that you didn't want to take it again. She offered to stay after school and help you review, but you told her you didn't feel like it. Is it starting to come back to you?"

"That old bag," Arnold says.

"Bag or not, you had a choice, and you made it. I want you to remember that. Because nobody did anything to you to keep you from graduating. This is something you did all by yourself. You and nobody else. Because that Constitution test is the bottom line."

Arnold snorts. "You mean that rinky-dink test . . ."

"They told you then. I tell you again. In this state you cannot graduate from elementary school —or junior high, in this case—without passing the Constitution test. Most of the other things can be gotten around. With the work that you did at the hall and at the other schools, you have enough credits to graduate, as long as you pass everything this quarter. But nobody can graduate without meeting the Constitution requirement."

"That's it, then," Arnold says.

"Two ways to go, Arnold. You can go ahead and not graduate, or you can try to learn enough to pass that test."

"Yeah. Well, I don't know any of that stuff. That old bag Evans made me stand in the corner just about the whole year."

Ms. Karnisian gets up from her desk and pulls

her hair away from her face. "It's your ballgame," she says. "If you want to take the test you'll have to make an appointment with Mr. Kelley, the social studies chairperson. And you'll have to take the test when the eighth graders do—in a week or two. But it's up to you. Nobody's going to make you do anything." She gathers up her books and then puts all the notebooks into a cardboard box. "So, I found out what you wanted to know, and it took me every spare minute out of the past twenty-four hours. I know that words escape you when you try to express your undying gratitude."

"All right," Arnold says. "I would have said thanks."

"But I didn't have all weekend."

"All right," he says. He looks over at me and then back at her. "Thanks for checking it out for me."

Ms. Karnisian smiles. "You're welcome, Arnold. You know I mean that, don't you? You know that you're welcome to ask something else if you need it, don't you?"

Arnold smiles and looks down at the floor. "Yeah, I know that."

"Good," she says quickly. "One piece of advice, and this is for free. If I wanted to learn something in a hurry, I'd get Warren Cavendish to help me."

Arnold nods and heads out the door. I follow after him. "Thank you, Ms. Karnisian," I say.

"Thanks for nothin'," she says and laughs.

When I come out the door, Arnold is already at the end of the corridor. He is trotting along, not looking back.

NINETEEN

MAY 19—MAY 25

"COME ON, ARNOLD," WARREN SAYS. "IT'S NOT ALL that tough, and you have all of us working for you."

"But I don't know any of that junk, man."

"But you will. Not a lot, but enough. Look, don't you even remember taking the Constitution test?"

"Not really."

"It's nothing but a one-hundred-question test—all true and false. So what do you need to know? You need the answers to forty questions. Then you can guess at the other sixty and get half of them correct. That gives you seventy right answers, and you pass. So all you need to know is forty things."

"But, man, I don't know forty things about anything."

"Look at this word," Warren says. "It's 'bicameral.' Say it over and over. Bicameral. Bicameral. It means that there are two houses, two parts of the legislature. But remember *two*. Bi—like bicycle. Bi—for two. Bicycle—two wheels, two cycles. Bicameral—two houses."

"Hey, man. Bicycle. That's how it got its name, huh? Two cycles?"

"Forget that. Remember bicameral—two houses. Worth a point on anybody's Constitution test."

"Okay," Warren tells him. "Start memorizing the things on these flashcards that Michael's been making."

"Forget it, man. There's no way I can do that."

"Look, those are amendments. They're on all the tests. I have them summarized in six or seven words each, and Michael has them all copied out in his crummy printing."

"At least you can read it," I say.

"Look at this one, Arnold. See? Number thirteen —no slavery. You can learn them."

"Oh, man, I'll just forget 'em again."

"Of course you will. That's what everybody else does. Right after the test you can forget all of it. Any other time, if you want to know about an amendment, you look it up in a book. But for this test, you memorize."

"It's not worth it, man. I'd rather not graduate than try to memorize all this stuff."

"Too late, Arnold, old buddy," Warren tells him. "I told you it was dumb when we started, but you asked us to help anyway. Now that we've done all this work, you're not going to quit."

"Executive branch," Harry announces. "Keep thinking 'X is the president.' See? X for executive."

"Don't bother with that," Warren mutters, without looking up from the pamphlet he's going through. "You know what an executive is. He's a big shot, a president. Save the memory tricks for the hard stuff."

"X is the president," Arnold whispers. "X is the president."

"Here's a poem," Jennifer says. "It's called 'Length of Terms': A congressman serves two; a president serves four; a senator serves six; Supreme Court forevermore. It's a rhyme, see?"

"Sure," Harry shouts. "Put some music to it, and we can all dance."

"Say it again," Arnold tells her. "Slower."

Warren shakes his head. "Look, for now a veto means no. If the president doesn't like a bill, he vetoes it. Forget about pocket vetoes. That kind of stuff is frosting. You don't need an A this time. All you want to do is pass. If we get time, which we probably won't, we can go back to things like pocket vetoes."

"Now you're talking, man. A veto means no."

"I've got an idea," Arnold tells Warren. "You go in and say your name is Arnold Norberry and take the test for me."

"Oh sure. They'd never suspect a thing. Except for about eighty pounds, we're practically twins."

"You think I'm gonna pass?" Arnold asks us.

"Of course you'll pass," Warren says. "You knew

more after the first night than most of the eighth graders ever know."

"Will he pass?" I ask Warren.

"He might. I figure he can probably get thirty right on his own. He knows more than that, but he gets mixed up. If he knows thirty, he only guesses at seventy. If he guesses half, he gets sixty-five. But he might be a lucky guesser."

"Oh, man, I should have talked to Mr. Kelley before," Arnold moans. "I just didn't want to see him until I was sure about taking the test. Now it turns out I have to take it on Friday. That gives us just one more night. I thought I'd have more time."

"That's great," Warren shouts. "It's the best break you could get. You're ready for the test right now. This way, you won't have to worry about forgetting any of it over the three-day weekend."

TWENTY

FRIDAY, MAY 26

IT'S 8:15, AND WE'RE ALL STANDING IN A CIRCLE in front of Mr. Kelley's room. Arnold is scheduled to take the Constitution test with Mr. Kelley's first period social studies class, and we're all there to cheer him on. Our little party isn't going well for one simple reason—Arnold hasn't arrived.

The eighth graders come past us, some of them walking very casually, others still glancing at their books. One boy has things written in pencil all over his fingernails. "Maybe we should have tried that," Harry says.

"Not a chance," Jennifer says. "I had Mr. Kelley last year. Right after he passed out the test, he walked down the aisle and checked everybody's hands and sleeves and desk."

"I didn't really mean it anyway," Harry says.

Margaret looks over at me, and I shrug. Nobody seems to have anything to say. It's a warm morning, building toward a hot day, but we stand around hunched over, the way people do in the middle of winter. Warren keeps walking to the drinking fountain and back. Sometimes he drinks, sometimes he just rinses off his hands.

"Do you think we ought to call him?" Harry asks. "Maybe he overslept."

"He doesn't have a phone," I say.

"That's all right," Harry says. "I don't have a dime."

Margaret comes up to me. "Do you have that old feeling?" she asks.

"I don't know. What feeling is that?"

"That old feeling that things are bad and going to get worse."

"I'm starting to get it."

Warren marches back from the drinking fountain. "He'll be here. He wouldn't dare *not* be."

Nobody answers him. The first bell rings, and more of the eighth graders come down the hall. "Did you study last night?" one of them yells.

"Heck, no. I didn't want to break my record."

"My brother says to mark everything you don't know false. He says there are always more false ones."

As the hall begins to empty, I look at Warren. "What do you think?"

"Give him a minute. He'll be here. He has to be."

Mr. Kelley turns the corner and comes toward us, carrying a large stack of tests. He watches us until he's right in front of us, as if he figures we're up to something. He stops and says, "The first bell rang some time ago. You'd better get going to your classes."

We take a few steps up the hall, enough so that Mr. Kelley goes on into his room. Harry keeps looking at his watch. "I don't know what happened," I say, although I have a sneaking suspicion that I do.

"Forty-five seconds to the bell," Harry says. With that, we all scatter for our classes. I look over my shoulder just before I turn the corner, in case Arnold has made it at the last minute. The hallway is empty.

TWENTY-ONE

FROM THE NOTEBOOKS
Assignment: What I will do (or would like to do) this weekend

ELVIRA PORTALUPE: THIS WEEKEND MY FAMILY is going on a camping trip, the way we do every Memorial Day. We have a travel trailer called a Fifth Wheeler, and we are going to Lake Pillsbury, where we will waterski, if it is warm enough. . . .

Jeff Garrison: This weekend I would like to go to San Francisco and watch the Giants whip the Dodgers three straight games. But I don't have any money, and I don't have any way to get to San Francisco, and the Giants probably won't win all three games anyway. (I'd settle for two out of three.)

Harry Beech: I am going to Oakland to visit my mother and meet the guy she just got married to. What I would like to do is haul Arnold Norberry back to Juvenile Hall and leave him there. What a rat!

Jennifer Kirkpatrick: Right now I think I would like to sleep until Tuesday. This year has gone on too long. It's hot and stuffy in here, and the air conditioner has been broken for over a month now. I'm tired of the whole thing.

Margaret Olson: This weekend I will sit in front of a fan and read while my mother grades term papers. She always put them off until Memorial Day weekend and then has a grading marathon. What else can I say? The fan we have at home cost less than ten dollars, and it works fine. Maybe you could pass the word to Mr. Bellows.

Michael Parker: I would like to get on my bicycle and ride so far from Hendley that I would need a roadmap to find my way back. I'll try to write some more later. Right now I just don't have anything to say.

Warren Cavendish: This weekend I am going to sit down and try to figure out what makes a person like Arnold Norberry tick. My father talks about some people being born losers, but I didn't know what he meant until I met Arnold. It would have been all right with me if he had taken the test and failed. But not to take the test at all is the sign of a real loser.

I'm disappointed and disgusted and just plain mad about all the time I put in. I know more about the Constitution right now than I did last year when I took the test. I'm not going to let it end this way. Arnold may be a born loser, but I'm not.

TWENTY-TWO

TUESDAY, MAY 30

I'M STANDING OUTSIDE MY FIRST-PERIOD CLASS when Arnold walks by and asks what's happening. We talk for a minute about how hot it's going to be by afternoon, and I wait for him to say something about Friday. When he keeps rattling on about how crummy it is that the coolers never work, I finally can't stand it any longer.

"All right," I say. "What happened to you on Friday?"

"I got sick, man. You know how it goes."

"You blew it. You could have passed that test easy."

He takes a step backward. "Don't get all excited, man. It's no big thing. I'm not worrying about it."

"Right."

The day turns out to be blah. Nobody is involved. I hear two teachers talking during pass period. One says we ought to end school before the Memorial Day holiday. "We do," says the other one. "It's just that we have to come back and go through the motions for a couple of weeks." That sums it up.

I come into English class a minute early. Warren is standing by the door and motions for me to join him. "It's surprise party time," he says.

"What's going on?"

"Just follow the leader, Michael. You can't give away anything if you don't know anything. We're going to fix things up."

We stand in the doorway and watch the class come past. "What are you doing?" Margaret asks me. "Practicing to be a butler?"

Arnold and Harry come in just before the bell, and Warren stops them. "Come on," he says. "Put down your books and let's go. We have to go to Mrs. Scott's room to get some textbooks. They're pretty heavy, so we need at least four guys."

"Sure," Harry says, tossing his books into the corner. "We don't want to hurt our backs."

We're just outside the door when the last bell rings. It's strange walking down the quiet corridor past the rooms full of people. Warren has our pass, and it's all legal. But it's still strange.

"This is all right, man," Arnold says. "How long's that pass good for?"

"Forget it," Warren says. "We go straight for the books and straight back."

Mrs. Scott's room is at the far end of the wing. We're just outside her door when Warren stops and grabs Arnold's shoulder. "This is it, Brother Arnold. They're taking the Constitution test in there, and you're going to join them. You go in there and do the best you can. If you flunk it, you flunk it. But as long as we spent all that time on this, you're not going to chicken out on us."

"Come on, man," Arnold says "What're you trying to prove?"

"Just read the questions carefully," Warren says. He sticks a pencil in Arnold's shirt pocket as Harry opens the door. Warren shoves Arnold through the doorway. "You can do it, champ," he whispers.

"Shhh," Mrs. Scott says.

Even though we spend most of the period writing, I keep thinking the clock must have stopped. When we finally get out of class, Arnold is leaning up against the wall, just across from the door.

"How'd it go?" I ask.

"No big thing, man." But then he can't hold it in. He comes toward us while he shouts, "You know what? The third question on the test was 'bicameral.' I don't know how you knew it, Warren, but it was there."

"It's always there," Warren says.

"Well, I saw that one and got it right. And then I went back and looked over the first two again. And then I went on. Some of that stuff—I don't know. But there was a whole lot that I knew. I mean, there were questions just like things you asked me."

"Did you pass?" Jennifer asks him.

"I don't know. I might have. I knew a lot of that stuff. Just a minute, all right?" He goes into the room, and I hear him telling Ms. Karnisian about "bicameral" being on the test.

"I don't know how you managed it, Warren," Margaret says, "but you did a whale of a job."

"What did you expect?" Warren asks, but he's smiling.

Arnold comes back out of the room with Ms. Karnisian, who goes off down the hall. "You know what she's gonna do?" says Arnold. "She's gonna see if there's any way we can get my test corrected."

The others have to go on, but Warren, Jennifer, and I stand in the hall and listen to Arnold while he goes over all the questions that he can remember. He wants us to tell him whether or not he got them right, but he garbles them so badly that we can never be sure.

Every minute or two Arnold does a switch. First he's sure he'll pass, and he's saying how dumb it was to worry about it. Then he starts talking about the words on the test that he couldn't understand, and he's saying that if he'd only known, he could have studied the whole weekend. And then he tops it off by saying, "No big thing."

When Ms. Karnisian comes walking down the hall, Arnold goes running to meet her. He doesn't yell or anything. He just runs right up to her. Then after they talk for a second, he turns around to us. At first I think he failed, but I see that Ms. Karnisian is smiling.

"Eighty-two," Arnold yells. The sound echoes in the empty corridor. "I got eighty-two."

"No big thing," Warren says.

TWENTY-THREE

POEMS TO ARNOLD

Assignment: Write a poem to be read aloud during the Arnold Passed Party to be held during the last fifteen minutes of class. (No poem, no cake.)

ELVIRA PORTALUPE: You struggled hard and
       passed the test.
You faced the task with zeal
       and zest.
And you succeeded. I am
       glad
To think of all the fun you
       had,
For you have learned the
       lesson well:
To win, just try. You'll do
       just swell.

Jeff Garrison: Orange is the carrot and
Red is the beet.
How could you pass and
Not even cheat?

*   *   *

Harry Beech: Now that you've passed,
                       You've sealed your fate.
                       You'll wear a robe
                       And graduate.

Margaret Olson: The study's over.
                       You passed the test.
                       Familiar words
                       Explain it best:
                       Plop. Plop. Fizz. Fizz.
                       Oh what a relief it is!

Jennifer Kirkpatrick: Hurray for you!
                       I knew you'd pass.
                       Smartest guy
                       In the whole darn class!

Michael Parker: My poems are lousy, stale
                           and slow.
                       I cannot get the words to
                           flow.
                       And yet some effort I must
                           make.
                       I'll die without a piece of
                           cake.

Warren Cavendish: A dashing young man
                           named Norberry
                       Passed a test about which
                           he was wary.
                       He made eighty-two,
                       Which he never could do
                       Without help from me, Jen,
                           Mike, and Harry.

TWENTY-FOUR

WEDNESDAY, MAY 31

THE ARNOLD PASSED PARTY GOES JUST THE WAY
it's supposed to. There's enough cake for seconds,
and everybody has a poem to read. Arnold starts
out being cool about the whole thing, saying, "Look
man, all those simple-minded eighth graders
passed. Why shouldn't I?" But when the poems
start, he doesn't kid around as much, and I think
for a minute that he's going to cry. He doesn't cry,
of course, and the whole party is a success.

Except for one thing.

Jeff Garrison is kidding Arnold, saying, "Aw,
Arnold, you weren't supposed to pass. You were
supposed to come back next year and keep Ms.
Karnisian company."

Ms. Karnisian laughs and says, "That's all
right. It wouldn't have done any good. I won't be
here anyway."

"Where will you be?" Jennifer asks her.

Ms. Karnisian smiles and shakes her head. "I
wish I knew. I've sent out over four hundred
letters so far, but nothing has come through yet.
Keep your fingers crossed for me."

Jeff starts teasing Arnold about the system he used for cheating, but I don't pay attention. I'm still thinking about those four hundred letters.

After class I stay around and help clean up the room. When the others are gone, I ask Ms. Karnisian again, "You mean you don't have a job for next year? No job at all?"

"Not a teaching job. I still have my job at the juvenile hall."

"But you'll get a teaching job, won't you?"

"I hope so, Michael, but it's a rough business."

"You mean, after all those years of going to college and then driving here every day and teaching for free, you could end up not being able to be a teacher?"

"Sure. That's happened to a good many people. It's a fact of life. There are more people who want teaching jobs than there are jobs. That means that somebody won't get one."

"But you're . . ." I stop because I don't know how to finish it.

"Thanks, Michael. Thanks for caring. Who knows? Maybe I'll get lucky. I've been doing all I can to help out my luck, though."

"But it's not fair," I say and then catch myself. She looks at me and laughs. "I know. You don't have to say it again—life isn't fair."

"Things aren't as bad as all that," she says. "I have a teaching job this summer at something called a street school—the Martin Luther King Memorial Street School in San Martin. Unfortunately, I don't get paid there, either, but at least I'll be teaching. And I still have a chance for a job this fall. Some districts hire over the summer. I'm still in there fighting."

"Well," I say, "I hope you make it."

"I do too," she says and winks at me as I head for the door.

I walk along the empty hallway and try to make sense out of it, but it's beyond me. You're a good teacher, you write four hundred letters, you drive a hundred miles a day in a beat-up old car to teach for free, you even teach for nothing all summer, and you end up with no job. Things shouldn't be like that. If life isn't completely fair, at least it ought to be a little bit fair. A person ought to have a chance. Instead, it's the old King Kong business all over again—the whole world ganged up against one poor monkey.

TWENTY-FIVE

SATURDAY, JUNE 3

ON SATURDAY AFTERNOON ARNOLD AND I ARE riding bicycles. He has my sister's ten-speed, which she never rides and doesn't care about until I want to borrow it. Today, before we can use it, we have to sign an agreement saying that we'll fix anything that goes wrong while we have it, even if it isn't our fault.

We go first to Harry's place. At 1:30 he's still in his pajamas, watching the ballgame on television. As soon as the game is over, Arnold and I try to talk Harry into going for a ride with us, but there's a vampire movie on Channel 2, so he won't budge.

After stopping at the A&W, Arnold and I are riding back toward my house when he turns off the main road into a subdivision called Westbrook Estates. All of the houses there are two-story jobs with big chimneys and double front doors. In the middle of the second block Arnold starts slowing down, and I move up beside him. "What's the matter? Bike not working right?"

"Don't get excited, man. I'm just taking it easy for a while."

He turns right at the corner, and I suddenly

realize that Jennifer Kirkpatrick lives down this way. I start to mention it to Arnold and then realize that he may already know it.

Jennifer is out in front of her house cutting some roses for a bouquet. "Arnold, Michael," she shouts as she runs across the front lawn. We stop and lean our bicycles against the hedge. "What're you guys doing?"

"Just doing the old fresh air and exercise bit," Arnold says.

"We were over at Harry's place," I say. Arnold and Jennifer are looking into each other's eyes, and I might as well be speaking French for all they'd notice. I turn away from them and see Jennifer's father standing in the driveway. "Hello, Mr. Kirkpatrick."

Mr. Kirkpatrick has been waxing this car of his. It's one of the first Thunderbirds ever made, but it looks brand new. He waves a rag at me and says hello. After looking at us for a minute, he puts the lid on the can of wax and walks toward us with these little short penguin steps. "Jennifer," he says, "I don't believe I have met your friend."

"Daddy, this is Arnold," Jennifer says. "Arnold, this is my father."

Arnold reaches out a hand, but Mr. Kirkpatrick doesn't seem to see it. He nods his head and says, "Hello, Arnold."

"How do you do?" Arnold says, pulling his hand back slowly. "That's a real nice car. What kind is it?"

"A Thunderbird," Mr. Kirkpatrick says, as if the question is a little stupid.

"Yeah. Well, it's a real nice car."

"Would you guys like some lemonade?" Jennifer asks us. "Come on inside, and I'll make some." Arnold and I follow her up the sidewalk and through the front door. Mr. Kirkpatrick stands and watches us go.

Jennifer leaves us in the entrance hall while she runs to get a vase for the roses. "Oh, man," Arnold says to me, "I can't believe this place."

I've been to Jennifer's a few times for parties, so I don't pay much attention until Arnold says this. The house is mostly antiques—the kind painted white with gold trim around the fancy edges. There are glass cases everywhere, full of cups and saucers and little statues. It's the kind of house you can look at and know right away that no boys live there.

When Jennifer's mother comes to meet Arnold, Mr. Kirkpatrick is with her. Mrs. Kirkpatrick says hello to Arnold and then asks me how my mother is and what grade my sister is in now. Mr. Kirkpatrick just stands back and watches Arnold and me. We're wearing our old jeans and sneakers, and Arnold's shirt is unbuttoned, the way it usually is. I guess we look funny here among the teacups and white furniture.

While Jennifer goes to make lemonade, Mr. Kirkpatrick takes us into the living room. Arnold and I sit down on this straight-backed couch that is just as uncomfortable as it looks. Mr. Kirkpatrick asks me about my father and about our vacations plans for the summer. Then he turns to Arnold.

"Are you a neighbor of Michael's?"

"No," Arnold says. "I live in the middle of town."

"Where?"

"Not too far from the hospital."

"Vincent Street?"

"Collins," Arnold mumbles.

Mr. Kirkpatrick keeps looking us over. He's smiling, but somehow I feel guilty of something—I don't know what.

"What does your father do, Arnold?"

"He's a scientist," Arnold says quickly.

"A scientist. That's interesting. What is his specialty?"

"He does a little bit of everything."

"I see. Where does he work?"

"In San Francisco. My parents are divorced."

"Do you go to visit him?"

"Sure," Arnold says, "I go whenever I can. He lives in this neat apartment that has a beautiful view. We go all kinds of places, all over the city."

"What's your favorite place?"

Arnold looks around for just a minute. "That's hard to say. I like everything." Then he says, "The Golden Gate Bridge. That's my favorite."

"I know San Francisco quite well," Mr. Kirkpatrick says. "I lived there for a number of years. Where is your father's apartment located?"

"He just moved out. He decided to buy a house after all these years. I haven't even seen it yet."

Mr. Kirkpatrick starts to ask again about the address of the apartment, but Jennifer comes in with the lemonade. After that she does most of the talking. She tells her parents about things that have happened in school and about people in our English class. Arnold and I sit on that hard couch and drink our lemonade.

As soon as our glasses are empty, Mr. Kirkpatrick stands up. "Maybe you boys would like to come out and see my automobile." We stand up and follow him outside. He walks us around the car once, telling us that this is a classic. I nod and try to look interested. I'd like to have a little car like that, but I don't really feel like hearing him talk about it. When he says something about the line of the trunk, I reach out and start to run my hand over it. "Don't touch it," he says disgustedly. "You'll get fingerprints on it, and the oil from your hands is hard on the paint."

When we have made our circle of the car, he walks toward our bicycles. "It's good to see you again, Michael," he says. "It has been nice to meet you, Arnold." He stands and watches us as we get our bikes and say good-bye to Jennifer.

Arnold and I ride for a few blocks without saying anything. After we leave Westbrook Estates, Arnold pulls over to the side of the road and stops. As I pull up beside him, he says, "I'd like to teach that fat jerk a lesson. I'd like to fix him good."

"Don't let him get to you," I say. "That's just the kind of guy he is."

"He didn't have to treat me like that. I'm just as good as he is. He's got no right to look down his fat ugly nose at me. He's not any better than anybody else, even if he has a car that's different and a big fancy house."

"Forget him," I say. "He's not worth it."

"That's easy for you to say. He was all right to you."

"Sure he was. Did you hear him when I almost put my finger on his precious car?"

"I'd like to pour sugar down the gas tank of that car. Or maybe just work it over with a hammer. Or just take a screwdriver and put some grooves in that fancy paint job of his. It'd serve the fat toad right."

"Forget it," I say. "That's just the way he is— rotten. He's not worth bothering about."

Arnold pushes off and starts riding again. "I'm gonna fix him, Mickey. You wait. Big high society barfbag anyway."

TWENTY-SIX

FROM THE NOTEBOOKS
Assignment: Discuss something you found out recently.

JEFF GARRISON: I FOUND OUT THAT MR. BELLOWS isn't as good a guy as I thought. I got into a fight at noon hour last Thursday with a kid that called me a dirty name. Mrs. Scott took us both to Mr. Bellows's office. He didn't even let me explain. He just said that if we couldn't behave ourselves, we couldn't go to school here. He suspended us for the rest of the week and called our parents to come and get us. That's why I was gone. Did you miss me?

Harry Beech: I think I am going to throw up. I never thought I would wish we had school in the summer, but I do now. I found out last night that I have to spend the whole summer with my mother and my stepfather. I just met my stepfather on Memorial Day, and I didn't like him much.

Here I had a neat summer all planned out. I was going to lie around and watch TV and go to the Municipal Plunge whenever I felt like it. Now I have to go live in Oakland in an apartment. I don't like Oakland or apartments or my stepfather. I think I will stop writing before I get sick.

Margaret Olson: (Confidential) I don't like to talk about things like this in my papers, but I need to say this to somebody. I may go back and cross it all out afterwards. What I really want to say is that Michael Parker is driving me absolutely stark raving mad.

For weeks I have thought he was going to ask me to go to the graduation dance with him. I know that he likes me better than any other girl at school. And at Marshall Martin, everybody (and I mean everybody) goes to the graduation dance with somebody. It's not like a big date or anything. Everybody is already at school for the graduation ceremony. But then after the chairs get put away and the dance starts, everybody is there with a partner.

Today at noon Michael and I were walking down the hall, and he asked me if I was going to the graduation dance. What was I supposed to say to that? I felt like saying, "Not unless you ask me, stupid." I just told him that I didn't know yet, that I hadn't really decided. And do you know what he said? He said, "Yeah. I haven't really decided either." Then he started talking about algebra, and we never did get back to talking about the dance.

So I will probably stay home from the dance because Michael never got around to asking me. I know that he was leading up to it, but somehow the whole thing got off the track.

Meanwhile, I think I'll go mix myself an arsenic milkshake.

Michael Parker: (CONFIDENTIAL) I found out something today that everybody else probably knows already. When you start thinking about asking somebody to go somewhere with you, everything changes. There's a girl I know that I have always gotten along with, and I was going to ask her to go to the graduation dance with me. (Everybody here has a partner at the graduation dance.) But I didn't know for sure if she was even interested in going. And I didn't know if somebody else had already asked her. So I got started talking, and everything got hard. All of a sudden, it was like I was talking to somebody I'd never met before. Always before, she and I could talk about anything.

The funny thing is, as soon as I decided to forget the whole thing and stay home from the dance, then we talked just the way we used to. But in some ways I wish I had asked her to go to the dance.

Elvira Portalupe: I just found out that I'm going to the graduation dance after all. I had never really considered it. Every year the teachers tell the students that everyone should come to the dance, with or without a partner, but almost nobody comes without a partner. Some people might, I guess, but I wouldn't.

Not expecting to go to the dance, I hadn't thought about it especially, although our home-making class has been working on the decorations and planning all of the refreshments.

But today at noon hour Harry Beech came over to where I was standing and asked if I would go to the dance with him. I was so shocked that I could hardly get the words out to say yes. And do you know what he said? He said, "Good. I was afraid that a cute girl like you would already have a partner." Then he went off. Do you know what? That is the first time in my life that a boy my age said I was cute.

This essay is running all over the place, but I am still excited. (Maybe you could tell that.)

Warren Cavendish: Here is a problem that I have been given this week: Do I go to Hendley High School next year, or do I go to a special preparatory high school three hundred miles away? My parents say that I'll have to make the final decision, but I don't think they could decide anyway. As they see it, Hendley High is a weak school, and they have picked out a boarding high school that has things like a computer terminal for students to work with. The teachers are exceptional, the classes are small, and the students are gifted.

My parents keep talking about whether it would be better for me to be with students of all levels or with an exclusive group. Should I have democracy or competition?

The silly thing is that the real problem has nothing to do with things like democracy and competition and computer terminals. The real problem, which never gets mentioned, is that I'm the only kid they have. I may not be much to look at, but they have gotten used to having me around. They don't know if they want me three hundred miles away, and I don't know if I want to be that far away. Instead of talking about this, however, we go on and on about computers and competition.

TWENTY-SEVEN

TUESDAY, JUNE 6

As I come down the hall to English, old Miss Kellaher is standing outside the classroom door. I've only seen her a few times since Ms. Karnisian took over the class, and I've forgotten how old she looks. Or maybe this has been a rough spring for her.

It turns out that Ms. Karnisian has a final exam at her college, so Miss Kellaher is back with us for the day. "Now, class," she says when she has finished taking roll, "I think it would be a nice idea if we had a little party for Miss Karnisian on Friday. Don't you think so? She has been a very dedicated student teacher, and I think it would be a nice gesture." We haven't said anything, but she acts like the vote is over.

"Who brings the goodies?" somebody yells out.

"You do whatever you think is best," Miss Kellaher says. "If each of you girls would bring cookies or a half dozen cupcakes. I think it would work out nicely. Would you like to do that? I'll bring the punch myself, and there are some paper cups and plates left over from the open house. Now, all we need is a present. I think a present would be nice, don't you? Just a little something to show our appreciation."

"You're gonna have to pay for it," Jeff Garrison shouts. "Everybody here is broke."

"Well, I certainly intend to contribute. All of you bring whatever you can afford tomorrow. Perhaps if one of you would like to be treasurer, that person could collect the money and buy the present. Don't you think that would be a good idea? It's easier to have one person in charge." I see her looking down the aisle at me, and I slide down in my desk. "Michael Parker, would you like to be treasurer?"

"No," I say, but everybody is yelling "Sure" and "He'll do it." So I end up being treasurer.

Then Miss Kellaher has us all write poems for Ms. Karnisian. She has heard about the party for Arnold and figures the same thing will work again. "Just write a little poem," she says. "If you need help with a rhyme or something, I'll be happy to help you."

Right away Warren asks her for a word that rhymes with "orange," and she spends a long time trying to think of one before she gives up. Warren, of course, is just putting her on, but Miss Kellaher thinks he is serious. "Maybe you could change the words around, Warren."

"I have mine already," Jeff Garrison yells out. "It's a little short, but it's really good. You want to hear it?"

"All right," Miss Kellaher says. "Read your poem."

Jeff stands up and clears his throat. "I call my poem 'To Miss Karnisian.' Here it is: 'So long, King Kong.' How about that for a poem?"

Everybody claps. Miss Kellaher takes Jeff out into the hall. While she's gone, some people throw paper airplanes out the window. I sit around and try to come up with some sort of poem, but everything I can think of is sappy and dumb.

In the middle of the period Miss Kellaher stops by my desk and says that she and I will go downtown right after class and pick out a present. Before I can think of an excuse, she is headed across the room to stop somebody from shooting rubber bands.

I sit there disgusted. Even if I didn't have anything to do, I wouldn't want to go looking for a present with Miss Kellaher. And I was planning to catch Margaret right after class and ask her to the graduation dance.

The whole shopping trip turns out to be a joke— a sick joke. To start with, Miss Kellaher leaves school just before the buses come, so the whole school is standing around as we drive past. Some of the guys yell stuff at me: "Now we know how Parker gets his grades." "She's a little old for you, isn't she, Mike?" "Boy, Parker really can pick 'em, can't he?" Miss Kellaher doesn't seem to hear any of it. I scrunch down in my seat as far as I can, and she lectures me on my posture all the way to the middle of town.

It turns out that Miss Kellaher already has the present picked out—a set of books by Jane Austen

(whoever she is) with lots of old-fashioned pictures. The only problem is that she lets me nose
around Bagley's Book and Stationery Store for half
an hour before she tells me this. I keep finding
books that would be all right, and she keeps giving
me reasons why they wouldn't be suitable. I guess
she's hoping that I'll come up with the right books
sooner or later. When she finally gives up and
shows me the Jane Austen books, I say that they'll
be fine. I'd agree to anything, just to get out of
there. "You go back and ask the class," she says.
"If they think you've made a good choice, then
you can go ahead and get them."

When I see that the books cost twenty dollars,
I try to go for something cheaper, but she says
that she'll put up whatever we can't raise. "We'll
be lucky if we can scrape up five," I warn her.

"Oh, I'm sure that our treasurer will do better
than that."

She offers to drive me home, but I've already
heard enough about my posture. I make up an
excuse about having some shopping to do and
then walk home.

Just as we are finishing supper, the telephone
rings. As usual, my sister jumps up and runs to
answer it. She comes back and uses her most
disgusted voice to tell my father that somebody
official wants him. Whenever the telephone isn't
for her, she acts like the victim of a plot.

"Who is it?" my father asks.

"I don't know. Somebody that mumbles. Deputy

Somebody or Other." She looks over at me. "What kind of trouble are you in now?"

When my father comes back to the kitchen, he says that he has to go downtown. He starts for the door and then turns back to me. "You might as well know. Arnold's mother has been arrested. The police say that if I come and get Arnold, he can stay here instead of going to a foster care center or whatever they call it. The man I spoke to figures that she'll be released in the morning."

"What did she do?" I ask.

"I don't know. What difference does it make? Go do your homework before Arnold gets here."

I go to my room and finish my algebra problems, but I keep thinking about Arnold. I wonder how I would feel in his place, but nothing will come to mind. I can't even imagine what it would be like in his place.

When Arnold comes into the kitchen with my father, my mother has a big plate of food waiting for him. He says that he isn't hungry, but once my mother gets him to the table, there's nothing wrong with his appetite. I sort of wander around, leaving him alone while he eats.

Afterwards, he and I go to my room. We lie on the bed and think about playing Monopoly, but we don't get around to it.

"You know what happened?" he says. "My mother was coming up the street, and somebody at the store started making fun of her. She went right after them, and then she got into it with the woman that runs the store. Then the cops came.

It was stupid, Mickey. Those lousy bums around there. If they'd just leave her alone, she wouldn't cause any trouble."

"That's too bad," I say, not knowing what else to tell him.

"I thought for a while they were going to take me over to San Martin to this place called Nuestra Casa. That's where I got put last time. I begged them not to. I mean it, man. I got down and begged. I kept telling them that I was going to graduate in a few days. Finally I asked if they would call my uncle and have him come get me. They went ahead and called your dad and never even asked him if he was my uncle."

"I'm glad they let you come."

"Me too, man. Usually on a D and D my mother is out the next day, but you can't tell."

"What's a D and D?"

"Drunk and disorderly. Usually they let her go the next day. The only thing is, she hit one of the cops tonight. If he wants to get her for resisting arrest or assault on an officer, she could be in there for a while. And I can't go back to San Martin now. Not now. You know what happened today?"

"Something else?"

"Something good, man. This is different. I asked Jennifer if she'd go with me to the graduation dance, and she said she would. Can you believe it? Man, I gotta stay around now."

"That's great."

"Yeah. Me and Jennifer at the dance. Wow!"

He turns his head and looks at me. "What about you? Are you going to the dance?"

"I don't know. I haven't decided yet."

"Come on, man. You oughta go. You know what you oughta do? You oughta ask Margaret. She's kinda cute."

I really don't want to talk about it. "I'll see."

We lie around for a while and watch a spider run around the ceiling. Then he says, "I tell you, Mickey, one of these days I'm gonna take off. It's just too much sometimes. I mean, man, look at it. There I was tonight, begging that cop not to haul me off to some foster care place, and I hadn't done anything. Not one thing. I tell you, man, one of these days I'm gonna take off and go."

"Where?"

"Canada, man. That's the place. Things are different up there. There aren't so many people, you know, and it's easier to get a job. I was talking to this guy at the hall, and he was telling me what it's like. He says that anybody that wants to work can get a job and make good money. Man, I could go up there and get my own place to live, and I could handle things all by myself."

"It's a long way," I say.

"What's the big deal, man? You get a car, you can get there in a day or two."

"Sure, but where are you going to get a car?"

He sits up and looks at me as if he doesn't know me. "You're so dumb sometimes, I can't even believe it. You must have spent your whole life sitting here in your room. Getting a car is about the easiest thing in the world. I'll tell you, man, we could go walking down your street here, right in front of your house, and I'll bet we wouldn't go a whole block before we found a car with the keys in it. I'll bet you that in half an hour we could find ten cars with the keys in them. We could just take our choice."

"And win a free trip to juvie hall," I say.

"Not if you're careful, man. Back in San Martin, me and this other guy used to go out for rides. We didn't take any chances. We'd just drive the cars for ten minutes or so and leave them. Even if somebody saw us take the car—which they never did—we'd be out of the car and gone before the cops came around. You just gotta know what you're doing."

"If you say so."

"Well, I say so, man. The only thing you'd have to be careful about is gas. You'd have to get a car with plenty of gas in it, so you wouldn't have to stop right away. Gas is kind of tricky. Cops keep an eye on service stations, and if they see you getting out of a car that doesn't look like it's yours, then you've got problems. What you have to do is stop at places with self-service pumps and pick your spot. You could be in Canada in no time."

"Canada's a big place," I say. "Bigger than the United States. Just whereabouts in Canada would you go?"

"Don't worry about it, man. All right? Just keep it cool."

"Besides," I say, feeling worse all the time, "think of all the fun you'd miss here."

Arnold looks at me for a minute, then grins. "I'll tell you one thing I'm not gonna miss out on. That's the graduation dance. Me and Jennifer. Oh, man, I wish it was tonight."

But pretty soon he's talking about his mother again, and he says, "It would be so much easier if I just went someplace and started over. You know, just got a job and a place to stay."

"But after graduation," I say, trying to get him back into a good mood again.

"Right, man. After graduation. And after the dance. Especially after the dance."

That night after the lights are out, I hear him moving around. He's on the rollaway bed, and I think maybe he isn't comfortable. "What's the matter?" I ask. "Having trouble getting to sleep?"

"No big thing," he says. "I was just thinking about something. Could we turn on the light for a minute?" I reach over and flip on the lamp and blind myself. "I want to use your calculator for a minute, all right?"

"Sure," I say. "It's over with my books."

"Don't worry, man. I'll put it back when I'm done."

"I wasn't worried," I say, rolling over to get away from the light. "Turn off the lamp when you're finished, all right?"

"Sure, Mickey. But, first, tell me something."

"What?"

"How far is it to Canada from here?"

I don't have a very good idea, and I'm too sleepy to get up and hunt for the atlas. "About eight hundred miles, I guess."

"Thanks, man."

I lie there and listen to him tapping on the calculator until I can't stand it any longer. "What're you doing anyway?"

"Just figuring," he says.

"Figuring what?"

"About Canada. If you had a car that got twenty miles to the gallon, you'd only need forty gallons of gas to get there. That means maybe two stops."

"I'll remember that," I say, pulling the covers up over my eyes.

I go to sleep with him still pecking away.

TWENTY-EIGHT

WEDNESDAY, JUNE 7

WHILE MS. KARNISIAN IS OUTSIDE ON HALL DUTY, I dash around and collect what money I can. I have a paper sack, and most of the people toss in something. When Ms. Karnisian comes inside, I go back to my desk. The sack is fairly heavy, but most of the coins are pennies. Harry comes in as the bell rings and hands me a dime.

"Don't spend it all in one place," he says.

"You figure you can afford the whole thing, or do you want change?"

"That was my last dime," he says, "and I owe my dad four bucks already."

"You and everybody else."

"I hope you picked out a cheap present, Treasurer."

I don't even dare tell him how much the Jane Austen books would cost.

While Ms. Karnisian is passing out our notebooks and telling us about the final examination she took yesterday, Miss Kellaher comes into the room. She says something to Ms. Karnisian, who nods, puts down the notebooks, and heads for the door.

"Now, class," Miss Kellaher says as soon as the door closes, "we have to hurry while she's gone. Michael, you go around and collect money from everyone."

"I got most of the money already," I tell her. I move up and down the rows, but nobody has much to add.

"Michael selected a very nice present," Miss Kellaher is saying. "He selected a set of books by Jane Austen, one of the world's great authors. I'm sure you'll be proud to give the books to Ms. Karnisian, won't you?" A couple of people mutter things, but nobody says anything out loud. "All right then, Michael. You can get those books today."

"I can't do it," I say. "I have a dentist appointment." This is an out-and-out lie, but I've had enough. Somebody else can try to buy a twenty-buck set of books with a sack full of pennies.

"Is anyone going past Bagley's Stationery?" Miss Kellaher asks. "Dottie Williams, don't you go that way?"

"Oh, all right, I'll do it," Dottie says to me. "Just write down the name of the stupid books."

I scribble the name of the books while Miss Kellaher talks about the refreshments. After I give the paper to Dottie, I raise my hand. Miss Kellaher calls on me after she has finished explaining about the cupcakes.

"Miss Kellaher," I say, "we don't have enough money for the present." I set the sack of money on Dottie's desk and head back for my seat.

"I don't want this old sack," Dottie says. "And I'm not going in there and count out pennies. You come and take it back."

"Too bad," I say. "I just resigned as treasurer."

"Michael," Miss Kellaher says, "please bring me the sack."

"Tell the old bat to get it herself," Arnold mutters.

I take the sack from Dottie and carry it to the front of the room. Miss Kellaher picks up her purse and starts digging inside. "Now, class," she says, "I want you to understand what is happening. I am giving Dottie the money for the present. I can't really afford it, but I'm going to do it. Now I want Michael to go around, and I want each of you to put in whatever you can." I go up and down the aisles, feeling stupid. Everybody acts like I'm the one putting the pressure on them. I get a few more coins from people, and one of the girls puts in a dollar bill. Somebody tosses in a wad of chewing gum.

When I hand the bag to Miss Kellaher, she looks in and stirs the money around with her fingers. "You can do better than that. I know you can. I gave Dottie twenty-one dollars. That's right. Twenty-one dollars. So I will be making up the difference between what you have in the sack and the twenty-one dollars. I know you want to be fair, and I know that you want to do your best for Ms. Karnisian."

So I end up making another trip around the room. I pick up almost nothing this trip. Miss

Kellaher looks into the sack again and shakes her head, but Ms. Karnisian is coming, so I get saved from another trip. Miss Kellaher just says quickly that all those who forgot their money can bring it to her tomorrow.

While I'm supposed to be writing in my notebook, I keep looking across at Margaret and trying to think of how I'm going to ask her to the dance. It should be easy enough, but it isn't. I think about writing her a note, and I even get out a piece of paper, but that turns out to be just as hard. I never get beyond deciding whether to write "Dear Margaret" or just "Margaret."

When class is over, I see Margaret start up the aisle and realize that it's too late again. I sit and gather up my books and call myself names. I'm still sitting there when she comes back into the room. For once, Ms. Karnisian has gone out the door and taken Elvira Portalupe with her. The last clump of girls moves into the hall, and Margaret and I are left alone.

While Margaret comes toward me, I start stuffing things into my binder. "Hey," she says, "school's over. You don't have to sit there any longer."

"Right," I say. I gather the last of my papers and stand up. She's looking straight at me, and I turn back to my desk, as if I'm checking to be sure I have everything.

"Michael," she says, "do you have something you want to ask me?"

I know what she means, but I can't get started that easily. "I don't know. Like what?"

"You're impossible. Like what do you suppose? Like would you like to go to the graduation dance with me? How about that for a starter?"

"Yes, I would," I say. "I thought you'd never ask."

"Come on. That's not fair."

"Says who? Anyway, you already asked me, and I accepted. You can't take it back now."

"Okay," she says and starts to grin. "But it's nobody's business who did the asking, all right?"

"It's a deal," I say.

We walk out of the room and find Ms. Karnisian standing all alone in the hall. I can't help wondering if she went outside on purpose, but how would she know?

I walk with Margaret out to the front of the school, where her mother is waiting. After they leave, I take off running to catch Arnold, ignoring all the people who turn and stare.

Later on, we find out that Arnold's mother has been released from jail, but she doesn't go home. My father takes Arnold and me by the apartment after supper, but nobody is there. Arnold wants to stay there by himself, but my father says he's responsible for Arnold until his mother is back home. So Arnold hunches down in the backseat and doesn't say anything more to anybody.

When we get back to our house, Arnold and I

stand around by the car after my father goes
inside. "I can't believe him," Arnold says. "I mean,
man, I spent half my life staying by myself. What's
the problem now? What's he think—I need a baby-
sitter?"

"That's just the way he is," I say, not sure
whether I'm sticking up for my father or not.

"Hey, man," Arnold says, "let's take a walk. I
want to show you something."

"Okay," I say. "Just a second." I go through the
garage and yell that we're going to take a walk.

"I can't believe you," Arnold says. "You can't even
take a walk without asking your mommy first?"

"Come on. I didn't ask. I just told them where
we were going."

"How come?"

"How do I know how come? It's just the way we
do things. No big deal."

Arnold laughs, although I don't see anything
funny. We go two blocks down without saying anything. Then as we turn the corner, Arnold walks
around one of the cars that is parked at the curb.
"Not that one," he says, coming back to the sidewalk. He circles the next car and the next. "Shut
out three times in a row. Hard to believe."

The next car in front of us is a green station
wagon with a big dent in one rear fender. Arnold
pats the dent and says, "Looks like they hit a
building. Probably backed right into it." He moves
around the car quickly. Before I realize what he's
doing, he's sitting behind the steering wheel. He
leans over and rolls down the window on my side.
"Hey, man, want a lift?"

"Arnold, what're you doing?"

"Hop in, man. I'll give you a ride home."

"You're crazy. It's not even dark. Somebody'll see you." I look up and down the street, but things are quiet just then.

"Not if you hurry and climb in."

"No way." I can feel my knees getting tight. "Come on. Get out of there. If they look out their front door, they'll . . ."

Arnold reaches over and turns the key, and the engine roars. "See how easy it is. I told you there were cars all over with the keys in them. And look—this one has three quarters of a tank. We could easy go two hundred miles before we had to stop."

"Okay," I say. "You made your point. Now let's get out of here."

"Climb in, man."

"Forget it."

"Climb in."

"Come on, Arnold. I've lived around here all my life. Everybody knows me."

"But nobody's looking, Mickey."

"Come on. You made your point."

Arnold glares at me now. "Look, Mickey Mouse, you get in here. Just for a second. I want you to get in and sit in the seat. If you don't, I'm going to lay on the horn until somebody comes."

I try to laugh. "Come on, Arnold. That's dumb. You'll just get in trouble."

"And it'll be your fault. Just get in. I'm sick of listening to you. Just get in."

I stand there by the door and look up and down

the street. About a block away somebody is trimming a hedge. Otherwise the street is empty. "Let's go back—," I start to say, but the horn goes off.

I jump at the sound, then open the door quickly. The horn stops. "You didn't think I'd do it, did you?" he says.

I stand there on the sidewalk with my hand on the door. "You're crazy. Those people could look out the window any time at all."

"Get in and close the door," he says.

"Look, I'm not going to ride in this car. I don't care what you do. You can honk the horn until the cops come if you want to, but I'm not going to ride in it."

"I'm not going anywhere, man. I just want you to get in and close the door. That's all. I want you to get inside, shut the door, and sit here."

"Forget it."

"I won't go anywhere. I promise you. I just want you to get in and sit for a second. If you don't, I'm going to lay on the horn."

"What're you trying to prove?" I say. He raises his hand toward the horn, and I know he isn't bluffing. I take one more look up the street and then climb in quickly and ease the door closed. "All right? Are you satisfied now?"

Arnold laughs. "Lesson for you, Mickey. Here you are—sitting where you're not supposed to be. And nothing happens. The cops don't come. There's no earthquake. Nothing happens."

I sit there with my knees shaking. I keep thinking about how I would explain to my parents about this if somebody caught us here. I start to talk, but I have trouble keeping my voice under control. "You made your point. Now can we get out of here?"

"You're the boss," he says. He reaches for the gearshift. That's enough for me. I throw open the door and dive out just as the car pulls away from the curb. I land on my shoulder on the sidewalk and roll over once. Before I am on my feet, Arnold is standing beside me. The station wagon is ten feet ahead of where it was, and the motor is off.

"You're something, Mickey," he says. "You're really something."

"Just lay off. If this is your idea of a good joke, you're warped."

He laughs and heads back the way we came. I follow behind, watching him dance along the sidewalk.

When we've gone a block or so, he stops and waits for me. I walk right past him, and he runs to catch up. "Come on, Mickey. I was just playing around."

"You're sick," I say. "Just leave me alone."

He laughs and walks along beside me. "That was some dive you made. What did you think? Did you think I was really going somewhere?" I just keep walking.

When we get back to the house, my father offers to take Arnold by his place once again. I say that I have some homework to do. I don't, though. I just want to be by myself for a while.

When they come back, Arnold is not in the mood to talk, which suits me fine.

Things stay quiet until we're getting ready for bed. Then he says, "You take things too serious, man. I was just playing around."

"You play weird games."

"You're funny, Mickey. I never knew anybody like you."

"I never knew anybody like you either," I say. "But I don't make fun of you because of it."

He puts down his shoes and looks over at me. "Come on, man," he says quietly. "You take things too serious. Hey, man, let it go. Forget all that stuff, all right? Tell me about the dance. Here I am with a date for the dance, and I don't know anything about it."

"What's there to know? A dance is a dance."

"No way, man. A dance when you got a date with Jennifer is something else. What do they do? Do they have a band?"

"At Marshall Martin? You're kidding. No, they just play records."

"Good. Man, I'd hate to think what kind of rock band they could get at Marshall Martin. Records are better. Hey, did you ever dance with Jennifer?"

"I guess so."

"What kind of dancer is she?"

"How would I know? Good, I guess. All the girls are good dancers."

"Oh, man. I just thought of something. What about afterwards? I never thought about afterwards. Are we supposed to have a ride home for them?"

"Nah. Come on. This is still junior high. The parents are all lined up in their cars outside the gym. You'll walk out to the car with her, and that's it."

"Everybody does it that way, huh?"

"That's how they do it."

"You know what'd be neat? To have your own car. Man, wouldn't that be something? Just to be able to drive your girl home. Maybe stop somewhere for a Coke first."

"Yeah."

"I tell you, Mickey. What I'd like is a little T-bird like Jennifer's old man has. Can't you just see you and me taking the girls home in something like that? It'd knock the eyes out of the whole school."

"Just don't get serious," I say. "It'd be neat, but don't think about it too much."

"Come on, Mickey. Let a guy dream a little, will ya?"

After I turn off the light, we lie in our beds, and I tell him everything I know about the dance, which isn't much. He wants to know if refreshments are free, what kind of decorations there are, how many kids go. All I know about graduation dances it what I heard from my sister, and I never paid much attention. But it's fun to listen to Arnold get excited and laugh.

We've been quiet for a while, and I'm starting to drift off when he says, "I wonder where my mother went." I lie still and pretend to be asleep. I don't have an answer for that one.

TWENTY-NINE

THURSDAY, JUNE 8

AFTER BREAKFAST MY FATHER TAKES US TO
school, stopping by Arnold's place on the way.
Dad and I sit in the car while Arnold takes his
things into the building. Ten minutes go by, and
I start wondering if we're going to be late. Dad
finally checks his watch and says, "Why don't you
run up there and see what's keeping him?"

I get out of the car and climb the wooden steps.
As soon as I open the outside door, I know what's
keeping him. I can hear his mother yelling, "Don't
you talk to me that way. You just watch your
mouth." Someone is pounding on the walls, and a
man's voice is shouting, "Hold it down. We're
trying to sleep." I turn around and go back to the
car.

"Is he coming?" Dad asks.

"He's having a fight with his mother."

"Well, we know she's home anyway."

In a few minutes Arnold comes down the steps.
"I couldn't find my book," he says as he climbs into
the car. "My mother's home."

"That's good," Dad says.

"Yeah," I say, looking out the window at the Good Buy Market. There is a man asleep in the doorway.

All we do at school is turn in our textbooks and kill time while the teachers fill out inventory forms and check the books for ink marks. All the tests are over for ninth graders, and there's nothing left to do.

When I walk into English class, Dottie Williams says, "Here he comes," using this really disgusted voice. I look behind me before I realize that she's talking about me. "Come here, Michael."

I walk over to her desk, and she slaps an envelope into my hand. I open it and see money inside. "What's this?"

"You klutz. Why didn't you put those books on layaway or something?"

"What?"

"Those morons at Bagley's sold the books to somebody else."

"Don't tell me that."

"The woman said she was sorry but that it wasn't her fault. She said if you had put some money down and put the books on layaway, this wouldn't have happened."

"Terrific," I say. "Why didn't you just get something else?"

"You're out of your feeble mind. How would I know what to get? You're the one who was in charge. All you had to do was put them on layaway."

I take the envelope back to my desk. "No problem," Warren says. "Go get something else."

"Oh sure," I say, "Just like that. Go get something else."

"We have faith in you. Doesn't that warm your heart?"

"It gives me heartburn all right," I say. I have nothing better to offer at the moment.

"If you need help," Warren says, "you can go see Miss Kellaher." He laughs when I turn away from him.

Margaret and Jennifer come into class just before the bell rings. Margaret is carrying Jennifer's purse and books, as well as her own. Jennifer looks terrible. Her face is puffy and blotchy, and her eyes are red. Her hair is hanging in her face, and she doesn't even seem to notice.

Ms. Karnisian puts on a record of somebody reading a Poe story called "The Black Cat." I sit back and listen, but I can't help looking over at Jennifer once in a while. She has her head on her desk, but every little while her body gives a jerk.

When the record is over, Ms. Karnisian says that we can talk for the rest of the period. "Just keep it quiet enough so I don't get in trouble," she says.

Harry starts telling me about a movie he saw last night called *The Mummy's Curse*, but I'm only half listening. Jennifer has gone off into a corner with Arnold, and I can see her crying while she talks to him. Then he shrugs his shoulders and heads back to his desk. Jennifer rushes up to Ms. Karnisian's desk, says something, and goes out the door. Arnold scrunches down in his seat and looks up at the ceiling. Harry is explaining how the mummy was overpowered, and I nod whenever he stops talking.

When the bell finally rings, Arnold moves over beside my desk. "Hey, Arnold," I say, "what's the matter with Jennifer?"

"Chick's having a bad day, man. No big thing." I look at him, expecting more, but he's finished. "Listen, Mickey, I just had a neat idea for something we could get for old Karnisian."

"Good. I can use it. What is it?"

"Give me the money, and I'll get it this afternoon."

"It's a deal," I say. "What're you going to get?"

"Don't worry about it, man. It'll knock you out when you see it." He takes the envelope from me and moves up the aisle.

"Hey, thanks, Arnold. I was really stuck."

"No big thing, man."

Margaret has been standing by Ms. Karnisian's desk. After Arnold goes out the door, she comes down the aisle towards me. "He doesn't seem very upset," she says.

"Who's that?"

"Arnold. I thought he'd be really hurt."

"What do you mean?"

Margaret looks at me as if I've grown another ear. "Didn't he tell you about it?"

"I don't know what's going on. What's the matter with Jennifer?"

"She can't go to the graduation dance. Her parents are having a family party for her right after the ceremony. Of course, they didn't decide to have this party until they found out that Arnold had asked her to go to the dance."

"What a lousy deal. Arnold didn't tell me anything about it. I can't believe it—a family party on graduation night?"

"Isn't that crummy? That way, though, they don't have to talk about Arnold. They just pretend they're doing her a big favor, throwing a party for her. And if she doesn't like it, she's just being a brat."

As we come out the door, Jennifer is standing there. She looks even worse than before. She throws her arms around Margaret's neck and starts sobbing. "You know what he said? He said it was no big thing." She has trouble catching her breath. "He said there was another girl here that he wanted to take anyway."

THIRTY

POEMS WRITTEN FOR THE SURPRISE PARTY

JEFF GARRISON: Roses are red.
Violets are blue.
If they call me dumb,
I'll put the blame on you.

Elvira Portalupe: Kind,
Agreeable,
Reads a lot,
Nice,
Independent,
Successful,
Intelligent,
And
Never gives up.

Harry Beech: When I miss this class,
Here's what I'll do—
I'll watch the movie
On Channel Two.

Margaret Olson: If you are sentimental,
If you regret our partin',
Then here is how to start

Forgetting Marshall Martin:
Don't think of what we've
    written;
Don't think of what we've
    spoken;
Just think of all that driving
And coolers that were
    broken.

Michael Parker: Maybe today
You should have stayed
    home.
It wasn't worth the drive
To hear this poem.

Warren Cavendish:
(To be sung to the tune of "Jingle Bells")
Writing all week long,
It makes my poor head ache.
I'm glad that school is done
Before my fingers break.
We started with a thud,
And then it soon got worse.
If it had gone another day,
I'd ride home in a hearse.

(Chorus)   School is done. Time for fun.
Let's all say good-bye.
First one here that sheds a
    tear
Gets hit with a lemon pie.

THIRTY-ONE

FRIDAY, JUNE 9

IN MY BINDER I HAVE SOME WRAPPING PAPER AND ribbon that my mother gave me, but I have a sinking feeling that we aren't going to need them. Harry tells me that Arnold wasn't in their math class, and he isn't around at lunch hour.

But a part of me keeps hoping. Even as I sit in Ms. Karnisian's class and watch everybody sneaking refreshments into the room, I find myself thinking that Arnold is still going to come through the door just as the bell rings. He'll come down the aisle with that half-dancing walk of his, set the present on my desk, and say, "No big thing, man."

The final bell rings, though, and Arnold doesn't walk in. Ms. Karnisian closes the door and sits down on her desk. She has to know that a party is planned. There are boxes and paper sacks on half the desks. She waits for a minute or two, sort of playing with the roll book, to give us time to do whatever we have in mind. Then when nothing happens, she gets out a book and starts talking about a man named Whittier.

The door opens, and Miss Kellaher marches in.

"It's time for a party," she shouts. Ms. Karnisian smiles and closes the book. Miss Kellaher looks at me and nods. I slide down in my seat and look away. "Michael," she says, "you can go ahead now." I shake my head, but Miss Kellaher is no longer looking at me. "We'll begin the party with a speech from Michael Parker." She begins to clap, and some of the others pick it up.

I stand up because there's nothing else to do. The speech in my pocket is all about wanting to give her something in return for what she's given us. It doesn't fit very well, now that we don't have a present. "Ms. Karnisian," I say, "things haven't worked out exactly the way we planned. We collected money to buy you a present, but the present hasn't gotten here yet."

Everybody turns on me at once. I can hear people all over the room saying, "Where is it?" and "What happened to it?" And over everybody else I hear Dottie Williams saying, "You klutz."

"I don't understand this," Miss Kellaher says.

"I'm sorry," I say. "I thought it would be here." I sit down, and I can feel a whole classroom full of people wishing they could take me out and use me for a punching bag.

"Well," Miss Kellaher says, "I don't know what to say. This has been a surprise for me, but we do have refreshments and poems to read."

"Then let's have a party," Ms. Karnisian says. "I've been waiting all year for these people to bring in some goodies to bribe me. I thought they'd never get around to it."

The girls lay out a punch bowl and paper plates

full of cookies and cupcakes. Everything is fine except for the stupid missing present.

After everybody gets refreshments, we read our poems. Warren sings his poem to the tune of "Jingle Bells." Then Jeff Garrison and Ms. Karnisian sing it with him. They sing it over several times, and everybody joins in on the chorus. When the poems are all finished, people line up for more refreshments. I go back to my desk. I don't know what I want at this point, but it isn't a cupcake.

Warren wanders back toward me, carrying a handful of cookies. He offers one to me, then eats it when I shake my head. "I'll bet I can guess what happened."

"Never mind."

"Isn't it an amazing coincidence that the present isn't here and neither is Arnold?"

"Never mind," I say again and turn away.

Ms. Karnisian is all over the room, laughing and joking with everyone. She comes back by my desk and says that she wants to talk to me after class. "I'm sorry about the present," I say.

"I'm not worried," she says. "Just leave your IOU on my desk."

When the period is finally over, I make a beeline for the door. I'm sick of the questions and the dirty looks and the sarcastic comments. Ms. Karnisian calls out to me, and I remember that I'm supposed to talk to her. Dottie Williams comes past me and says, "That was really a nice party, except for one thing."

"I know," I say. "but we had to let you come because you were part of the class." She makes a face and keeps walking. About ten steps down the hall, she turns around and calls me a klutz again.

When everyone has gone past, I go back in the door. Ms. Karnisian is standing by her desk with Warren and Harry. I stand back, waiting for her to finish, but she waves me over.

"I wanted to tell the three of you," she says quietly, "that Arnold has had some problems. I don't know too much about it yet. All I know is that he was picked up in San Martin last night driving a stolen car. I haven't had a chance to talk to him yet, but I should be able to see him tonight."

The three of us look at each other. Harry lets out a low whistle.

"Obviously I don't want this spread around, but I wanted you to know about it. Arnold had a very positive experience here, probably the best of his life. I don't know what will happen to him now, but I know that he's much better off for the time he spent here with you boys."

Warren shrugs his shoulders. "Well, it was a good try anyway."

"What did you expect?" Ms. Karnisian asks with a sad smile. "He couldn't get eighty-two every time."

"This is so dumb," Warren says suddenly. "What was he doing in San Martin anyway?"

"I don't know. It wasn't easy for him here. Everything was very new. It took him a while, but he seemed to be doing so well. I thought he was really looking forward to graduation." She stops and shakes her head. "He *was* looking forward to it. I know he was. He was so proud to have passed that test." She looks at each of us. "But things happen, things that you can't plan for. It's bound to be an up-and-down fight. We had a wonderful up though."

I have kept quiet as long as I can stand. "When you see him, ask him about your present. He ran off with all the money we raised. Tell him thanks a whole lot from me." I turn and walk out of the room. After spending a whole hour feeling like a jerk because there isn't a present, I'm not ready to listen to any more talk about up-and-down fights.

As I rush out the door, Jennifer steps in front of me. The two of us are the only ones in the hall. "Michael," she says, "I want to ask you something."

"I'm in a hurry right now," I say, heading away from her.

She runs to catch up with me. "I'll walk along with you. I just want to know if . . ." She reaches out and grabs my arm. "Michael, do you know where Arnold is?"

I stop and look at her. Her hair is hanging across her forehead, which bothers me. I find myself wishing that she would start playing with it, the way she usually does. "Yeah, I know where he is, but I'm not supposed to . . ." I can't stand to have her look at me the way she is doing. "Oh, what difference does it make? He's in juvenile hall. He got picked up in San Martin last night driving a stolen car."

"Oh, no."

"Listen, Karnisian just told me. Don't say anything, all right?"

"I won't tell anybody," Jennifer says softly.

"Margaret says she told you about my parents and the dance."

"Yeah, she told me."

"Well, Michael, when you talked to Arnold afterwards, was he mad?"

"I don't know. He's hard to tell about."

"I really need to know."

"Look," I say, "I'm giving it to you straight. He didn't seem mad, but that doesn't mean anything. With him, you can't always tell what he's thinking."

"I wanted to go to the dance. I really did."

"So did he. That was all he talked about."

"But when I told him, he said there was another girl. . . ."

"Come on, Jennifer. What did you want him to do? Get down on the floor and cry and kick his feet? That's just the way he is."

"Something happened yesterday," Jennifer says. She looks down the empty hall and then back at me. "I don't know what to think about it. I thought maybe you could tell me."

"What's that?"

"You know my father's car—the special one, the Thunderbird?"

"Yeah, he showed it to us."

"Well, somebody broke into the garage yesterday and destroyed it. They slashed the tires and broke out the windows and smashed the lights. They even took some paint from the shelves and dumped it over everything. It was a terrible mess."

"That's too bad," I say, trying to keep my face from showing anything.

"Well, don't you see?"

"No."

"Don't you?" she asks, looking at me strangely.

"I don't know what you mean."

"Do you think Arnold did it?"

"Why?" I say, stalling for time. "Do you think he did?"

"I don't know. He might have. He might have wanted to get back at my father because of the dance. I just don't know."

"I don't see how he could have," I say. "Right after school he took off for San Martin."

"You don't think he did it then?"

"I don't think he could have."

"Well, thanks, Michael. If you hear any more about him, would you let me know?"

"Sure."

She goes off toward the main door, still shaking her head. I can't figure out whether she wanted Arnold to be innocent or guilty. Either way, I haven't helped her much.

For me, there's no mystery, of course. Maybe somebody will buy the coincidence, but I know better. I couldn't be any more sure if I had been standing there handing Arnold the paint cans.

I feel funny about the whole thing. It was a dumb move on Arnold's part. And it doesn't even do any good. A man like Mr. Kirkpatrick has insurance for stuff like this, so he isn't out much. And even if he didn't have insurance, he could probably just go out and buy another car like it anytime he wanted.

At the same time, I'm just warped enough to

smile when I think how Mr. Kirkpatrick didn't want me to get any fingerprints on his precious paint job.

But I still wish Arnold hadn't done it.

THIRTY-TWO

FROM the Hendley *Herald-Record*, Saturday, June 10

A CASE OF MISDIRECTED YOUTH?

A fifteen-year-old Hendley youth discovered Thursday evening that when a person veers from the straight and narrow path, he may wind up going the wrong way on a one-way street.

According to San Martin police, Patrolman John Torrez was traveling on San Martin Avenue when he observed an automobile that was being driven in an erratic manner. While Torrez had the vehicle under surveillance, it suddenly turned north onto Bailey Drive, which is limited to southbound traffic. Torrez gave chase and apprehended the driver.

A check of identification revealed that the car had been taken earlier in the day from a parking lot in Warner. The youth, a student at Marshall Martin Junior High School, is being held at the juvenile detention center in San Martin.

THIRTY-THREE

MONDAY, JUNE 12

THE LAST WEEK OF SCHOOL IS CALLED PLAY WEEK, and that's all we do. Our books have already been turned in, and we sit around in class and get people to sign our yearbooks. Because of graduation practice in the afternoon, our class periods only last about twenty-five minutes. Everything is relaxed and easy, but somehow I have trouble getting into the spirit of things.

Everybody's talking about Arnold. The article in the newspaper didn't give his name, but it might as well have. By Monday everybody knows about it, and the big joke is that Marshall Martin is such a rotten school that it doesn't even turn out good crooks. Ha ha. Or that we ought to teach driver's training here so that our graduates could handle the cars they steal. Ha ha again.

By the time I get to English class, I'm fed up with everybody. Several people want to know if I have the present, but I just shake my head.

Ms. Karnisian comes into the room and looks at us. "What?" she says. "I thought we were going to have another party today. Where are the goodies?" And then she laughs. "I want to thank you for the party on Friday and especially for the poems. I treasure them. I really do." She spends a minute or two with her roll book. Then she says quietly, "I saw Arnold over the weekend."

This gets a reaction—some questions, some laughing, some jokes. "Which way was he going?" somebody yells.

Ms. Karnisian waits until it dies down. "Arnold was very concerned about what happened, and he wanted you to know about it. I'm sure that most of you have heard that he was arrested. The whole school seems to know about it. If nothing else, I guess it shows that somebody reads the newspaper."

For a moment or two she doesn't say anything more. The whole class is quiet and waiting. Then she says, "I have a letter here from Arnold. He spent most of yesterday writing it. He asked me to read it to you, and I said I would if it appeared that everybody already knew about his troubles. And it certainly appears that way." She reaches into her purse and pulls out several sheets of binder paper. It takes her forever to get them unfolded and ready to read.

"Here it is," she says finally. " 'Dear Class,' he writes. 'I am back in juvenile hall because I did something stupid. Here's what happened. On Thursday afternoon Mike was stuck because the store had already sold the books he had picked out. So I decided I could get them at the big B. Dalton bookstore in San Martin. It's only fifty miles to San

Martin, and I figured I could hitch a ride over there, get the books, and be back home before dark.

" 'A guy in a pickup gave me a ride right away. He let me off in Warner, but I didn't care. I was already halfway to San Martin. But that was it. I couldn't get another ride. I stood there for hours, and nobody would stop. I've never waited that long for a ride in my life.

" 'I didn't know what to do. It was getting late, and nobody would stop. I decided to walk back to a truck stop. Sometimes if you stand around and ask, truckers will give you a ride. They'll never stop on the road for you, but sometimes you can talk them into taking you along.

" 'I was about a block from the truck stop when I saw a car with the keys in it. I didn't even think twice. I just climbed in. I figured I could get to San Martin, buy the books, and have the car back in Warner before anybody ever knew it was gone. It didn't work that way. The cops picked me up in San Martin.

" 'So I'm back in juvenile hall. I don't know for how long. I'm sorry everything turned out this way. The money for the present is in an account here at the hall, but I can't get it out until I'm released. Ms. Karnisian says not to worry about it, but I'm sorry I spoiled the party.

" 'That's about it, I guess. I'm sorry about the way things turned out, and I'm sorry that I spoiled things for everybody, especially me.' " Ms. Karnisian looks up from the letter. "He signs it 'Your Friend, I Hope, Arnold.' "

Everything is very quiet as Ms. Karnisian folds up the letter. Jennifer has her head on her desk, and nobody's looking at anybody else. Finally Margaret raises her hand and says, "When you see him, tell him we said hello."

Ms. Karnisian smiles. "You can do better than that. You have a few minutes before the bell. Write him a note if you feel like it. I'll take them to him."

While most of the people around me are scribbling, I sit and think about Arnold's letter. I wonder if I'm the only one in the room who doesn't believe his story. I can't help remembering what Arnold told me about confessing to something different than what people expect. Even so, I feel like I ought to write something to him, but it's hard to know what to say. After writing "Dear Arnold" on my paper, I'm stuck.

When the bell rings, the room empties in a hurry. It's now lunch hour by this week's schedule, and people are dashing out to beat the line in the cafeteria. I wad up my paper and toss it into the wastebasket as I go by.

"Still mad at him?" Ms. Karnisian says.

"It's just hard to figure out what to say."

The last of the people push through the door, and she and I are left alone in the room. "You got put in a rough spot on Friday," she says.

"Yeah, but it's not that." I can't find the words I want. "Look, I'm not really mad. I just don't know what to say to him."

Ms. Karnisian nods her head. "It's hard." She looks at me the way she might look at some animal that had been left out in the rain. I feel my throat getting tight, and I can't hold it back any longer.

"Look," I say, "the whole letter's a lie. He was mad because of his mother and because Jennifer's parents wouldn't let her go to the dance with him, so he suckered me out of the class money and took off." Even in the middle of this, I don't want to tell her about Mr. Kirkpatrick's car. "He had this dumb idea about running off to Canada. He thought he could get a job up there."

Ms. Karnisian doesn't look surprised at all. She just smiles at me and nods her head.

"So what do I say to him?"

"I don't know, Michael. You might tell him how you feel."

"That's the whole thing," I say, and I have to catch myself to keep from crying. "I don't know how I feel. There are just too many things at the same time." I take a couple of steps toward the door and then turn back. "The whole thing was dumb. He's going off to Canada, and I'll bet he doesn't even know where it is. All he knows is what some moron at the juvenile hall told him. With our twenty bucks, he thinks he's going to get to Canada and get a job. He's going to drive there in a stolen car, and he doesn't know where it is, and he doesn't know how to drive. That cop . . ." I stop because Ms. Karnisian is laughing.

"He's not exactly a master criminal," she says and laughs again.

"It's not funny," I say, although I catch myself starting to smile. "It's dumb, but it's not funny."

She holds her hands in the air. "It's dumb, all right. It's so dumb and so sad that you either laugh or you cry. Dumb as it was, though, Arnold is back in the hall, and he needs all the support he can get."

Suddenly I feel better, and things start to clear. "You know," I say, "it's weird. It doesn't really matter what he did. He did something dumb, and he got put back in the juvenile hall. It really doesn't make any difference whether he was running away to Canada or whether he was doing what he said in that phony letter."

"Not to me."

"Or me," I say. "It just took me a while to realize it." I reach into my binder for a pen. "Could you hang around for just a minute? I want to write a quick note."

THIRTY-FOUR

NOTES TO ARNOLD

Hey Arnold—

I hope to see you soon. I just hope you come back here to see me instead of the other way around.

> Hang in there—
> *Jeff Garrison*

Esteemed Arnold:

Greetings and salutations. Your absence from our ranks is regrettable. I trust that it is your intention to remedy the situation with all due haste.

> Best Regards,
> *Warren Cavendish, Esquire*

Dear Arnold,

How are you? Good, I hope. I guess you're going to have a lousy summer too. I have to go to Oakland this weekend. I guess it's better than Juvenile Hall though.

I hope you get to come back to school with us in the fall. I think Hendley High will be neat (especially after being in Oakland all summer).

> Your friend,
> *Harry*

Dear Arnold,

I felt really bad when I heard what happened. I know that you felt really bad too. What is it like where you are? I think about it, and I get scared. It must be awful.

I hope that you can come back to Hendley. It would be awful if I never saw you again.

Love,

Jennifer

Dear Arnold,

Hurry up and get out of there. We're all rooting for you, and we'll be here when you get back. Take care of yourself.

Mike (Mickey)

THIRTY-FIVE

THURSDAY, JUNE 15

IT'S A MUGGY, HEAVY EVENING, AND MY GRADUA-
tion robe hangs on my shoulders like a wool
blanket. We're standing in the teachers' parking
lot by the side of the gym, waiting for the signal
so that we can begin to march in. When we left
the cafeteria a few minutes ago, everyone was in
line. Now people are wandering back and forth,
waiting for something to happen. Some of the
boys have their hats off and are using them for
fans. People keep fussing with the hats, trying to
get the right tilt on them and trying to remember
which side the tassel should go on. Jeff Garrison
has his robe fixed like a cape, and he's playing
Superman.

A few parents are hurrying toward the main
entrance of the gym, but I don't think they need
to rush. The band has just started to tune up, and
that takes at least ten minutes.

I check my watch, a present from my parents,
and see that we're already four minutes late. Mr.
Bellows comes out of the gym and shouts for us
to line up. As the line forms again, he walks along

beside us. "Hats on now," he orders. "Stand proud. I want you to look like the successes you are."

Harry, who is right in front of me in line, says, "You know what? Last year a girl fainted during graduation, and it wasn't anywhere near this hot. I'll bet somebody faints tonight."

"I just hope it isn't me," I say.

We stand, more or less in line, and listen to the blats and squeaks of the band's tuneup. "Be sure to spit out your gum," Mr. Bellows says as he walks along. "We want you to look as grown up as you are."

The band starts to play that same old draggy song that gets played at every graduation, and Mr. Bellows shouts, "All right. Move around to the front door. Keep your places in line. Be sure to stand up straight and smile."

People begin to move through the door, and I walk forward, being careful not to step on Harry's robe. Mrs. Scott is standing at the door, holding each person back until the one in front has gone a certain distance down the aisle. She whispers, "Step, step, step" as she lets me go, but I never do figure out if I'm doing it right.

When everybody is finally inside, there is the flag salute and the invocation. Then we get to sit down, and I half listen to Mr. Bellows's welcoming speech while I try to see where my parents are sitting. When I finally locate them, my mother gives a little wave. She can't be listening very carefully either.

The first of the student speakers is a girl named

Natalie Nichols, who is covaledictorian along with Warren. Harry elbows me. "You know what? Warren is taking Natalie to the dance." I'm too amazed to say anything. "They were talking about the dance yesterday, and she kind of asked him."

"It doesn't matter who asked," I say. "I'm glad he's going."

I have heard Natalie's speech during the rehearsals, but I haven't paid much attention. This time, though, I'm listening as she begins, "A poet named Walt Whitman wrote, 'Afoot and lighthearted, I take to the open road, Healthy, free, the world before me, The long brown path before me, leading wherever I choose.' Like Whitman, we, the graduates of Marshall Martin Junior High School, face the open road that is our future, the long brown path that will lead wherever we choose. . . ."

"Oh sure," I find myself muttering. Natalie goes on talking about our standing at the beginning of a journey where all roads are open to us, but I've had enough. Sometime somebody ought to give a graduation speech about the way things really are. Somebody ought to mention that you can work for years like Ms. Karnisian and then not even be able to find a job. And somebody ought to talk about the choice of roads that somebody like Arnold has.

But then, just as I'm getting angry, I remember that at his last choice of roads, Arnold went the wrong way on a one-way street. I can just picture the whole thing. There's Arnold driving down the street—very cool and very careful. He's five miles below the speed limit and right in the center of the lane. When he spots the cop in his rearview mirror, he stays cool. He has to get away, but he can't draw attention to himself. He puts on his blinkers at the right spot and then makes a slow, careful turn—the wrong way.

"Hey," Harry whispers, "what're you smiling about?"

"Nothing," I whisper back. I don't think I could explain it, even if I wanted to.

"That's pretty funny all right," Harry says.

I kick his chair and grin. I still feel sorry for Arnold, and I still wish he could be here, and I still think there ought to be a truthful graduation speech sometime. But it's hard to stay angry. It's graduation night, and I'm going to the dance with Margaret.